A Name Earned

Tim Tingle

7th Generation
Summertown, Tennessee

Library of Congress Cataloging-in-Publication Data
is available upon request.

7th Generation
an imprint of Book Publishing Company
PO Box 99, Summertown, TN 38483
888-260-8458
bookpubco.com
nativevoicesbooks.com

ISBN: 978-1-939053-18-3

23 22 21 20 19 18   1 2 3 4 5 6 7 8 9

Contents

Contents

To Robbie Trujillo,
who has faced and overcome
tough life challenges and
"earned his name."

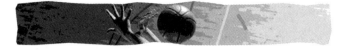

CHAPTER 1

Not Again

"It was an accident."

How many times have I heard that?

It was an accident.

From the time I was a little kid.

It was an accident.

Dad didn't mean to break my shoulder. Hoke, yeah, he might have meant to shove me down the stairs. But the stairs are carpeted, the floor is carpeted—what's my problem anyway?

It was an accident.

So Mom left, and I dug a hole in the backyard, behind a giant oak tree. I had to hide somewhere. I found an old wooden door at a nearby junkyard and somehow carried it home. I tossed it over our backyard fence, dragged it across the yard, and covered the hole with it. I glued leaves and grass and broken branches on top of the door, so it looked like our weedy and overgrown backyard.

Nothing more.

So I now had my very own secret backyard room. And since it was summertime and Dad didn't report me missing, I was free.

Yeah. Free.

All I had to do was keep away from Dad. With the help of my best friend, Johnny, I dug a small tunnel at the front of the hole, facing our back patio. I put a thick plastic pipe through the hole, so I could see and hear Dad when he sat on the patio, drinking and talking with his buddies.

But after a while, even his drinking buddies got tired of hearing him fuss about me—his only son, his only child, whom he hadn't seen for a week.

Then a month.

Then *who's counting*?

An impossible situation, right?

Wrong.

Basketball saved my life. And maybe being a member of the Choctaw Nation of Oklahoma had something to do with it, too.

"Always give thanks to the ancestors," Dad often said. "You remember them, they remember you." Yes, he drank his beer, but he was also proud to be Choctaw, and so was Mom.

And so was Coach Robison, the first American Indian *ever* to coach a sports team at our school. He was Choctaw too, and he wanted me to play on the team. Me! I had never played a game in my life, except on the playground. I spent hours on the outdoor court, every day.

To get away from Dad. And I'm not a big guy, but I can shoot a three-pointer. I learned to nail it from any distance.

I can dribble without looking at the ball. I can go left or right, so nobody can guard me by overplaying. You learn those things on the playground, where make-it-take-it rules. You lose, you sit down.

One evening, as I sat in my underground room, watching Dad and Coach on the back patio, Coach waited for Dad to set his drink down. The conversation went something like this.

"Byington," he said, "what would you say if Bobby played high school basketball?"

"I'd say you're crazier than I thought you were!" Dad shouted. "What kinda joke is this?"

"No joke," Coach replied. "You might not know it, but he shoots a three-pointer as well as anybody I've ever seen, this side of the NBA."

"And where did he learn to do that?"

"At the playground. At least that's where I saw him."

"So you're the new basketball coach, is that right?" Dad asked.

"You know that. Why are you asking?"

"Just to clarify something," Dad said. "If Bobby's disappeared, how's he gonna play ball? Though I gotta admit," he added with a laugh, "he'd be tough to guard if you can't see him!"

And that night I was in for the biggest surprise of my life. (Hoke, one of the biggest!)

When I was sure Dad had gone to bed, I climbed out of the hole and took a walk. Coach Robison was waiting for me, long after dark, when I climbed back into the hole. He told me an old Choctaw story about a young boy called No Name. Since he had not earned a name, his father was ashamed, and yelled at him, even shoved him—very much like my dad did to me.

At the close of the story, the boy dies while rescuing another Choctaw during a battle. But he returns—*in the body of another*—and his dad, ashamed of how he had been, spends the rest of his life making it up to his son.

When I first heard it, I hated the story. I cried and sobbed to hear my life in an old Choctaw tale. But the story gave me hope, so I took the biggest chance of my life. I told Dad about my secret room. Soon after that, I climbed out of my hole and returned to my bedroom.

And when school started, I became a starter on the high school basketball team, as a sophomore. I was the first American Indian to ever play on any sports team at the school. And I wasn't alone. My best friend Johnny, who's the son of a Cherokee lawyer, also made the starting five. He's tall and skinny and loves to rebound.

Then came real trouble. Dad showed up drunk at my first game and was thrown out of the gym. The night his son, his Bobby Byington, became the first Choctaw to ever step foot on the high school basketball court—and he shows up drunk!

After the game I followed him in Johnny's car, twisting and turning on the mountain roads, till I saw him standing by the roadside. His arms were stretched out to me. He was trying to say *he cared.*

I let go of the steering wheel and crashed into Lake Thunderbird. I came so close to death. Dad stood by my bed in the emergency room. Soon Mom joined him.

I was half conscious. Barely alive.

My eyes were glazed over, but I could see Mom and Dad standing together, for the first time in months. Dad looked at Mom, with tears streaming down his cheeks.

"I can tell you this," he said. "If he comes back to us, I will never touch another drink as long as I live. You have my word on that."

I did survive, and so far Dad has kept his promise. He has not touched a drop of liquor, and Mom has come home.

So when I hear "it was an accident," my life story speeds through my mind.

So here we are—today—returning from our first family picnic ever, and as we pulled into our driveway my Dad's phone rang.

"Are you there now?" he asked.

Mom and I looked at each other. We knew it had something to do with Lloyd, my teammate, or his dad. Now that my dad was walking the sober Choctaw road, Lloyd's dad stayed on Highway Drunk.

Dad hung up the phone, took a deep breath, and rubbed the back of his neck.

"Who was it?" Mom asked. "Is everybody hoke?"

"That was Coach Robison. And Lloyd's dad is back in trouble with the law. And he won't admit to anything! It was only an accident! That's what he keeps saying."

"Dad, please. What was only an accident?"

Dad covered his face and hung his head, almost like it wasn't true until he said it. "It's Lloyd's mother. She's in the hospital with a concussion."

"No!" Mom cried out. She fell into Dad's arms, and they hugged tight. "When will this ever stop?"

"When we stop believing it was an accident," Dad said.

Here I was, sitting in the window seat of Dad's pickup truck, watching Mom and Dad sob like little kids, hearing that another family had to go through what they—what *we*—had survived.

I am so proud to be part of this family.

Then my thoughts went to Lloyd.

"How's Lloyd?" I asked.

"He saw the accident," Dad said. "And his dad told him he better tell the truth."

"You know what that means," I said.

"I sure do," said Dad. "It means he better lie if he knows what's good for him."

"Where is Lloyd now, Dad?"

"He is at the hospital, talking to the cops. Coach is there, too. And he's asked me to come."

"Hon," he said, turning to Mom, "I've got to go."

"I understand," Mom said. "Just be careful. Hoke?"

"I will."

"And call us whenever you can. Please."

"I will. I promise."

"Dad?"

Mom looked at Dad. They knew what I was asking.

"Sure, Bobby. You can come. If you stay away from Lloyd till the cops say it's hoke. He needs a friend, but you can't get in the way."

"I promise, Dad. Yakoke. Thank you."

CHAPTER 2

The Accident

"You feel hoke, son?" Dad asked as we pulled into the hospital parking lot.

"I'm scared for Lloyd, Dad. What happens if they throw his dad in jail? Where will Lloyd go? To some foster home or state school? He deserves better than that."

"How about you and I make a promise, right now, before we step out of the car."

"I'm listening."

"Let's you and I promise to do everything we can to see that Lloyd stays in school, stays on the basketball team, and doesn't have to be afraid every day of his life. Agreed?"

Dad, my new Dad, was both a parent and a friend. He knew what to say and when to say it.

I looked out the window and took a long, deep breath.

"You alright with that, Bobby?"

"Dad, has anybody told you you're a pretty-good dad?"

"Has anybody told you you're a more-than-pretty-good son? Now, let's shake on it."

He reached out his palm, I took it, and we made our handshake promise. "Of course, neither one of us knows what that promise will involve," Dad said. He slammed his truck door and we headed to the emergency room entrance.

As we stepped through the door, we spotted Coach Robison. He sat alone at a corner table with a wrinkled brow and a tight, nervous look on his face. He stood up and motioned for us to join him. "Thank you for coming," he said.

"Any news?" Dad asked.

"Good news is that Mrs. Blanton's concussion is minor. She will be released later today."

"And Lloyd?"

"He's in an office around the corner, giving a statement to the police. His father insisted that he be present during the interview, even though

Lloyd is eighteen, old enough to talk without his parents' permission."

"Will he be safe at home with his dad, Coach?" I asked.

"Don't worry, Bobby. Lloyd is smarter than we thought. I guess he's had to be smart to survive this long. He told the police he wanted his dad to be present, to hear everything he had to say."

"Why would he say that?"

"Well, Bobby, I think he knows his dad will assume the worst, but if he's there during the interview, he will at least know the truth."

"Any idea what really happened?" Dad asked.

"Yes," Coach said. "I did have a chance to speak quietly with Lloyd. He told me his dad had gone several days drinking only a few beers and staying away from the bar. But he finally lost it this morning.

"He woke up mad, according to Lloyd. He threw his plate of breakfast eggs in the garbage and jumped in his truck. He must have driven to the corner store, and when he returned home an hour later, he was already staggering drunk."

Coach paused, and I looked at Dad. He was running his hand through his hair, as he always did when he was nervous. I knew he was replaying his own life of drinking and driving and blaming everybody else for his problems.

I touched his arm and he gave me a nod of thanks.

"And the missus?" Dad asked.

"Yeah. Mrs. Blanton," said Coach. "She was either mopping the kitchen floor or washing down the back patio with the garden hose. Take your pick. When the policeman pointed out to Blanton that he was changing his story, he claimed he was so upset he couldn't remember. He said she slipped and fell on the wet floor.

"That's when they turned to Lloyd. At first Lloyd said he wasn't there, but when an officer took him aside, he said he would talk if his dad could be there."

"And that's the last you heard?" Dad asked.

"Yes. Next thing I knew they ushered Lloyd and Mr. Blanton to the back office."

"So do you think he hit Mrs. Blanton?" Dad asked.

"No, I don't think so. There are no bruises on her face, nothing caused by a fist. Blanton insists she fell."

"It was an accident," I whispered. Dad shook his head, looking back and forth from Coach Robison to me.

"And even if it was," Dad said, "it was an accident caused by those terrible two B's."

I tilted my head and looked at Coach, waiting for an explanation.

"Bitterness and booze," Coach said.

"My dad makes nothing but A's, Coach. No more B's for him."

"See how lucky I am, Coach," Dad said, fist-bumping my shoulder. "Gotta love this kid."

A nurse stepped through the swinging doors and approached us. "Are you Lloyd Blanton?" she asked me. "Your mother is awake and asking for you."

"No, ma'am, I'm a friend of Lloyd's."

"Lloyd is talking to the police about the cause of Mrs. Blanton's accident," Coach said.

"Oh? She said she slipped and fell on her kitchen floor," the nurse answered, with a surprised look. "I was unaware of any issues.

So we are talking about possible domestic abuse?"

"We know nothing of that," said Coach. "You'll have to ask the officers."

With perfect timing two police officers, followed by Lloyd and his dad, entered the waiting area. "And here they are," Coach said.

"Mr. Blanton, I am the nurse attending to your wife. She has asked to see her son. That must be you, young man," she said, nodding to Lloyd. "Will that be all right, Mr. Blanton?"

"Fine with me. Go ahead on, son."

"We're here, Lloyd," I said quietly as he stepped by me on his way to the door, nodding hello and tapping his heart with his fist.

"Hey, Coach," he said.

"Say hi to your mom, Lloyd," Coach said. "Tell her we hope to see her at the next game."

"I will, Coach. Thanks."

As the doors closed, a silence wrapped itself around the waiting area. Everyone looked at the floor. Nothing Coach or Dad said or did would carry any weight. Mr. Blanton turned his back to us, facing the door to the parking lot. We were all waiting to see what the policemen would say.

"Mr. Blanton," said the sergeant in charge. "I'm sure you know you cannot drive home in your present condition. If it were up to me, I would arrest you for driving to the hospital under the influence."

He gave Mr. Blanton a stern look, daring him to reply.

Silence.

"I advise you to catch a ride with your friends and have someone else drive your vehicle home for you. Is that clear?"

"Yes. I understand."

The officer walked to the door, then paused and slowly turned around. He looked each of us in the eyes before speaking. "I wish I could believe this is the end of it," he said.

CHAPTER 3

Glass in the Shoulder

"Want to shoot some hoops, Lloyd?" I asked when he returned to the waiting area. I was trying my best to make this dark cloud fly away.

Lloyd looked at me like I was crazy, so I gave him a smile and shoulder shrug that said, *What else can we do?*

"Sure, Bobby. Your place or mine?"

"Well, since neither of us have a basketball goal at our house, how about the park?"

"Sounds good to me."

"Mr. Blanton, mind if I give the boys a ride?" Coach asked.

I never know where these dangerous and brilliant ideas come from. They always pop up in the middle of chaos. Like the idea to dig a hole in my backyard, and that crazy idea turned out all right. So why not try another one?

"Thanks, Coach. And maybe Mr. Blanton can come along too. Would that be hoke?" I asked, turning to Lloyd's dad. His eyes grew big, and he glanced at everyone, surprised to be included.

"Yeah, sure thing," he said. "Let me check and see when your mom is getting out. I need to be here for her."

He turned to the nurses' desk while Coach pulled out his phone to make a call. In five minutes tops, Lloyd and I were climbing into Coach's car.

"Can we stop by my house real quick and pick up my basketball?" I asked.

"Not necessary," said Coach. "I just called Johnny, and he's meeting you at the park with his basketball. I thought you might need one."

We all laughed, even Mr. Blanton, as we pulled out of the lot.

I glanced over my shoulder and saw Dad running his hand through his hair in that worrisome way of his. Since I'm pretty good at reading minds, especially where Dad is concerned, I knew what he was thinking. "Why did he do that? Why did Bobby ask Blanton to go with them to the park? Doesn't he know Lloyd needs to stay away from his dad?"

Lloyd doesn't need to stay away from his dad, I thought. *He needs to figure out a way to get along with him!*

Dad hung his head as expected, once more reminded of the hurt he had brought to his family. I wanted to jump out of the car and let him know that everything is different now. But that had to wait. Lloyd needed me now.

"I can't stay long," Mr. Blanton said. "I've got to get back to the hospital as soon as possible."

"Thanks for coming with us," Coach said.

"No prob, Coach Robison," he said, glancing at Lloyd, then me. "I'm still a little surprised you boys wanted me around. How come you asked me to join you, Bobby? Coach was gonna take you."

"I don't know," I said in a quiet, shy voice. No one said a word, and I decided it was time for me to tell the truth, the risky truth.

"Mr. Blanton," I said, "I wanted you to know that I trust you. I know you didn't mean to hurt

Lloyd's mother. And sometimes it's good to get away, even for a little while."

"What do you know about it, kid?" Mr. Blanton asked. He was growing angry, and I could smell the booze on his breath.

"I want to tell you about my dad, Mr. Blanton, when he was still going to the bar every day," I said.

We were approaching a stop sign, and Coach eased to a halt. He leaned forward and gave me a look that said, *You're either the bravest or the dumbest kid on the planet, Bobby Byington.*

"Please, Mr. Blanton, I mean no disrespect," I said. "I want to tell you about when I saw a different side of *my* dad. When I first saw that he cared for me."

Coach drove his car through the intersection without a word. I waited till we reached the park and he parked by the curb. He turned off the engine and we sat in silence.

"This happened last summer," I finally said, "the first day after Mom left. I was sitting at the table drinking orange juice for breakfast. Dad must have been mad, but he didn't say anything.

He walked behind me and jerked the chair so hard I fell backward and hit the floor.

"The juice glass shattered, and Dad slipped. He landed hard on his back, and I ran as fast as I could out the door. I knew he'd come after me. But he didn't. He fell on a big piece of broken glass, and it cut deep into his shoulder.

"I saw blood spurting everywhere, and I stopped. Dad looked at me in a way I had never seen him look at anybody. He pulled the glass out, still lying on the floor, and held it up for me to see. For the first time in my life I saw my father, looking at his son. That's all," I said. "I just wanted you to hear that."

We sat for a long moment without saying anything. Lloyd took a quick look at his dad. Mr. Blanton looked out the side window away from us.

"Go on and get out," he finally said. "Coach, can you take me back to the hospital?"

I opened the door and jumped to the ground, while Lloyd scooted over to follow me. "Wait, son," his dad said. "I'm not saying I'm easy to live with, but you know I did not hurt your mother. It was an accident."

"I know, Dad. I just hope she's hoke."

As Coach pulled away, I saw Mr. Blanton glance in the rearview mirror. The look on his face reminded me of Dad, lying on the floor with the glass in his shoulder.

CHAPTER 4

Mr. Blanton, Basketball Fan

"Some day today, huh?" Lloyd said as we walked across the park to the basketball court.

"Can't get much worse," I said.

We both thought about that for a minute, then smiled and shook our heads.

"You're right," I added. "It *can* get much worse. But not today. Can we agree on that?"

"As if it's up to us."

Suddenly Johnny pulled up, driving his bright-blue car, shiny and new. He rolled his window down and tossed a basketball in our direction. "Be back in fourteen minutes!" he yelled. "Time me!"

"Clock starts now!" I shouted, picking up the ball and waving thank you. As Johnny sped away, Lloyd and I slipped back into our conversation.

"So how is she?" I asked, instead of asking my real question, "What really happened?"

"They don't seem to be all that worried about Mom, so I think she'll be alright. She really did slip on the floor, like I told the cops."

I wanted to ask, "And your dad had nothing to do with it?" But I knew to wait. We reached the court and Lloyd took a few dribbles—with his left hand. He picked the ball up and tossed me a pass, still only with his left hand.

I caught the ball and let it fly.

Good sign! Nothing but net.

"Your three, my dime," Lloyd said. I tossed him the ball, and he tucked it under his arm. "Yeah, Dad was drunk, and Mom was trying to get away from him. I heard the noise in the kitchen and looked through the door just as Mom was falling. She tried to grab the table, but her feet fell out from under her."

He gave me a look and I patted him on the shoulder.

"You don't have to ask," he said. "Dad was on the other side of the table. He couldn't have shoved her. But he was mad and yelling, and he did reach for her. So was it his fault? Yeah. He doesn't come home drunk, she's not in the hospital."

"Thanks for telling me, Lloyd."

"Thanks for understanding."

We shot jumpers for a while, trying to get lost in the b-ball world and far away from the troubles of grown-ups. Soon Johnny arrived with a carload of Panthers, our basketball teammates.

Small guard Bart and high-jumping Jimmy flung the rear door open and ran to the court, ready to play. Tommy and Johnny walked slowly across the grass, looking tall and tough.

"We'll take Lloyd and whip you boys, three-on-three," Tommy said. "Think you can handle it?"

Hard not to laugh at him, but Tommy was a senior and he was trying halfway to be funny, so I decided to play along.

"Yeah, Tommy, we'll go for that," I said. "But Lloyd has to tie his left hand behind his back. Not fair otherwise. He's too good."

We all had to laugh at that, since Lloyd had just learned how to play with his left hand a few weeks ago, thanks to Coach Robison.

"Anybody need to warm up?" Johnny asked.

"Naw, Johnny," Tommy said. "Let's get it going. Let the boys have it."

He tossed me the ball and I moved to the top of the key. I gave him the ball, the custom in three-on-three, to make sure the defense was ready. He rolled it to my feet, which is not the custom.

"Guess we gotta school you, Tommy," I said. I tossed it in to Bart, who drove hard to the baseline, leaping up for a lay-up.

Not a chance, I thought. Bart stands a foot shorter than Johnny and Tommy, and they both stretched high to block his shot. But Bart is a senior, and he does know what the big men love to do on the playground—pound the ball with their fists and send it sailing through the trees.

Bart was ready. He faked the shot and flipped it over his shoulder to Jimmy, who soared to the basket for the bank shot.

"Whoa, Bart!" said Johnny. "You been watching some NBA?"

Bart had to be the shyest kid in school. He smiled and shrugged his shoulders. "Don't take no NBA skills to fake you guys out," he said.

"Yeah!"

"Dat's what I be sayin'!"

"You tell him!"

"Bart be *bad*!"

Nothing like playground basketball with teammates who get along, especially teammates who understand why we're here.

For Lloyd. To let him know we have his back, and whatever happens we're there for him. And so went the afternoon. Good basketball, lots of long, arching shots, decent defense but no *in your face.* No elbowing or taunting.

"It's all good," said Johnny, summing it up.

An hour later, Mr. Blanton pulled up. He parked his truck and rolled the window down. Jimmy grabbed the ball and held it. "Guess you gotta go, Lloyd," he said.

"No, not yet. Dad's parked," said Lloyd. "Let's keep playing."

Jimmy just stared at him, waiting for an explanation. But Johnny got it. He slapped the ball from Jimmy, and Bart scooped it up. He tossed it to me for a three-pointer from the corner, and the game went on.

"Hey!" Jimmy yelled. "I'm on your team, Johnny!"

"Not if you hold the ball. We're here to play."

Of course we weren't ignoring Mr. Blanton. We all watched him from the corner of our eyes, and we shared a common thought. *No big deal. Treat him like a normal dad. Who knows? He might become one.*

Mr. Blanton strolled across the park and settled at a picnic table near the court—the same table where my family had our first-ever family picnic, just a few hours ago.

Bart kicked the ball out of bounds and it rolled to his feet.

He picked the ball up and tossed it to Lloyd. No big deal. But just before Lloyd put the ball in play, his dad said, "In case anybody's wondering, she's fine and coming home soon."

"Hey, great news!" Johnny said. Jimmy, Tommy, Bart, everybody gave a shout-out to Lloyd. I high-fived him, and he smiled back at me. But it was not a normal smile. His mouth was tense, and I knew what he was thinking. *So now Mom is coming home. To what? More yelling, more drinking and cussing? She's fine now, but what happens next time? And there will be a next time. There is always a next time.*

"Thanks," Lloyd said. "Dad, we ready to go to the hospital?"

"We still have some time. They're prepping her now, doing a few more tests. Go on with the game."

I've never been so proud of my teammates. They knew why we were here—to support Lloyd. And how best to do that? Relax, leave all the troubles by the roadside, and as Mr. Blanton said, go on with the game.

And so we did.

Our ball, since Jimmy scored the last basket. I tossed it in to Bart. He took one dribble and tossed it back to me, setting a screen at the top of the circle. Jimmy fought for the rebound position under the basket, expecting me to launch another three-pointer. But Lloyd fought over the screen and slapped the ball out of bounds as it left my hand.

"Yeah!" Mr. Blanton hollered. When we all turned to stare at him, he grew embarrassed. "Oh, sorry guys. I guess playground basketball is a little different from games at the gym. I'm just doing what a dad does."

Even Lloyd had to smile. But I knew he also wanted to cry.

I knew how I would have felt. Part of me would be so happy that Dad was finally proud of something I did.

But another part of me would want to scream at him, "You are doing what a dad does? No way! What kind of dad sends his wife to the hospital? What kind of dad does that? And what kind of dad drinks so much his own son stays away, just to keep from getting hurt?"

We went on with the game, playing hard and tough. We made sure Lloyd earned every basket he scored, no giveaways. His dad would spot that in a heartbeat.

Lloyd bit his lip and hustled as hard as he did on the real court. I had to admit, I would not enjoy a game with this guy hounding me for four quarters. And he drove hard to the basket, scoring lay-ups and his now famous fifteen-foot jumper.

The big boys on his team, Cherokee Johnny and Tommy, let him take charge. They set picks for him. They fought for rebounds. And when he drove to the bucket, they waved a hand high, ready for the quick pass.

I glanced at his dad after every play. Sometimes he leaned back with his hands on top of his head. Other times he buried his face in his hands. From my own dad's experience, I knew what he was going through. He wanted so bad to be a good dad, to let his son know how proud he was.

But even more than that, he wanted his beer. He wanted to raise a can high and holler loud, surrounded by his drinking buddies. His body craved the booze while his heart wanted something else. Something he never knew. Not yet.

Two games later, Lloyd tossed in a ten-footer from the baseline for the win. Jimmy threw the ball high into the treetops, a sign that we were finished.

"Nice game," he said. We all shook hands, high-fived, shoulder-bumped, and turned to go.

Mr. Blanton stood and stretched. "Makes me tired watching you young men," he said. "Ready to go, Lloyd?"

"Yes, sir. Be good to see Mom."

"Tell her we said hello," Johnny called out as we jumped in his car. He started his engine, then did something really strange. He slapped the steering wheel with both hands, leaned back, and blew out two lungs full of hot air. Whooosh!

Then he said what we were all thinking.

"Did that really happen?"

CHAPTER 5

Game Day, Gotta Focus

Monday morning, as usual, Lloyd and I met at the gym before school. "Everything hoke at home, boys?" Coach Robison asked. "How's your mother, Lloyd?"

"No problems, Coach," Lloyd said. "Mom rested and Dad was cool. No more fussing."

"Good," Coach said. "Let's have an easy morning workout. No running. Save that for tonight. Twenty free throws, same number of jumpers, and ten minutes of dribble-drives with your left hand. That'll be enough for this morning."

Monday morning. The gossip in the halls and lunchroom was never-ending and full of lies— about Lloyd's dad and mom and fights and cops. That's all anybody wanted to talk about.

But not me.

"Game Day. Gotta focus."

That was my only reply, and it worked.

Lloyd heard me say it on the way to first period. He pulled me aside and said, "I'm gonna borrow that. Thanks."

By fourth period people were passing me in the hall and saying, in a deep voice, "Game Day. Gotta focus."

Everybody around would laugh and point and leave me alone. But it was friendly laughter. There was no making fun about it. By the end of the day I was giving high fives, and friends were strutting by and chanting, "Game Day. Gotta focus."

Nothing better, I thought. That's the old Choctaw way—survive with laughter.

Warm-ups over. Tension high. Coach Robison gathered us around for his pre-game talk. He glanced at me and Lloyd. I'd give a hundred dollars to have it on YouTube.

"Game Day. Gotta focus."

That's what he said. No more tension. We smiled and joined hands, a team again, relaxed and ready to roll.

"Hoke, boys," he said. "Back to work. I got a late scouting report on Union High, tonight's opponent. They're playing small ball this year. They've got a good post man, but he's mainly a rebounder and shot blocker. We'd better be ready for a full-court press. You know what to do, Johnny?"

"Yes, sir. Jimmy throws the ball to me around their free-throw line, and I hit Bobby or Lloyd."

"That's right, and it's gotta be fast. No picking up your dribble near the sidelines. They'll double-team and trap you there. Let's make 'em pay. Fast breaks and lay-ups. And maybe a three-pointer, but only if we've got rebounders. Are we ready?"

We nodded and joined hands.

Go Panthers!

The crowd was really into it tonight, from the opening tip.

Tigers got the tip, and the race was on. Jimmy hurried back and blocked a lay-up try, from over the shoulder!

But a Tiger guard snatched the ball and hit a short jump shot.

Tigers 2–Panthers zip.

Coach was right. We were facing our first full-court press since my return. And I watched from the bench. Jimmy ran up and down the sidelines looking to make the inbounds pass. He hit Johnny, who turned and flipped to Lloyd racing by.

A long pass to Darrell, who tossed it behind his back to Jimmy for a lay-up. "Good job!" yelled Coach. "Keep it fast!"

Tigers 2–Panthers 2.

Midway through the first, with the Tigers up by three, Coach motioned for me. "I'm putting you in with Lloyd. Let's beat the press, then slow it down, catch our breath, and run our half-court offense. You feel like a three-pointer?"

"I'm ready, Coach."

"Good. Let 'er fly, Bobby."

Let 'er fly? How often does a high school basketball coach tell a sub who enters the game with his team down to let 'er fly?

The next ball out, I took Bart's place. He was breathing hard and seemed glad to get a rest.

"Let's run the play!" Coach shouted from the sidelines. He waved his arms up and down, palms down, the slow-it-down sign.

Lloyd tossed me the ball, and I fired a pass to Johnny in the corner. He faked a drive to the baseline, and I drifted behind him. My man left me, going for the rebound. But Johnny didn't shoot.

Nope. He flipped the ball over his shoulder, without even a glance in my direction. I took two steps back, caught the ball on the first bounce, and let it fly.

No more tragedy, I thought, as the ball left my hand. *It's miracle time!*

The ball floated through the net to tie the game. My girlfriend, Faye, would be so proud of me. I thought of her as I hit my first three-pointer of the game. But it wasn't the last one.

Nope. Lloyd pulled a sly one. He turned to trot downcourt as the crowd cheered.

Panthers, Panthers! Go! Go! Go!

The opposing coach called out instructions to his team as the crowd cheered louder. Nobody noticed when Lloyd snuck back and stole the inbounds pass. He laid it in for two more points, and the fans went nuts.

Panthers, Panthers! Go! Go! Go!
Go home, Tigers. You're too slow!

We had our first lead of the game.

"Toss it inside," their coach shouted. "Go to the post."

As if we weren't listening. Jimmy and Johnny double-teamed their post man, slapped the ball away, and Coach's "slow it down" went out the window. Lloyd and I tossed the ball back and forth. I faked their lone defender off his feet and tossed it to him for the easy bank shot.

Panthers, Panthers! Go! Go! Go!

With everybody stretched from one end of the court to the other, Tigerman threw a long pass. For an easy bucket. Yeah. Easy if Darrell couldn't jump through the roof. He did, swatted the ball to midcourt, where I caught it on the run and launched another three.

Nothing but net.

This was a miracle times ten, and by halftime we had a fifteen-point lead.

"Everybody feeling good?" Coach asked at the half. The manager passed out water bottles, and we nodded "you betchas" and gulped it down. "I know the shots are falling, and everything is going our way. But don't think this game is over," he said.

"We're in good shape, and I'm proud of you men for keeping up the pace. But with this high-speed tempo, fatigue will set in. Anybody's lungs burning?" he asked.

No one wanted to be the first to admit what we all felt. "Free pizza to the first Panther to tell the truth," Coach said. "Anybody's lungs burning?"

Seventeen hands shot up.

We all had a good laugh. Coach sure knows what he's doing. Choctaw laughter one more time.

"You'll be fine with a little burning in the lungs," he said. "But don't let it get the best of you. When your legs stop running and you can't jump like before, wave to me and take a break."

CHAPTER 6

DAA, First Meeting

At the start of the second half, Coach pulled Lloyd and me aside. "Let's see what you two can do. You'll both be starting." He then spoke to the team as we tightened our circle around him. "No letting up," Coach said. "The shots were falling for us in the first half, but this game is not over yet. They'll expect us to try to slow things down, to take it easy and keep our lead." He knelt and motioned for us to come closer. "I want you boys to play as fast and tough as if you are *down* by fifteen points. Understand?"

"Yes sir, Coach," we all said, nodding and feeling fired up and ready to play. Our home crowd was ready, too. We gave 'em a show for the first two quarters, and they wanted more.

Panthers, Panthers! Go! Go! Go!

Johnny got the opening tip to Lloyd, who tossed the ball to Darrell streaking down the sideline. Darrell lobbed the ball to the basket, and Jimmy caught it with one hand and laid it in.

Panthers 40–Tigers 23.

As play continued, Lloyd and I let the big men take most of the shots. By the halfway point in the third period, we were up by twenty, and Coach whistled for a time-out.

"Nice job, boys," he said, as we joined him on the bench. "Let's see what our second team can do. Get after 'em, boys. Play good defense, run the ball, and hit the boards."

I found a seat on the far end of the bench, away from Johnny and Lloyd, my best-friend teammates. I took a swig of water, and for the first time all day, removed my mask.

My game-day, gotta-focus mask.

I searched the stands for Mom and Dad. And yes, my girlfriend, Faye. Faye was currently dealing with the bullying from Heather, a mean classmate. "Wow!" I whispered. I was so proud of my folks. Faye was sitting between them, Dad on one side, Mom on the other.

Faye held her box of hot buttered popcorn in her lap, and Mom and Dad helped themselves. They cheered and laughed and talked like they'd known each other for years.

Let's see Heather smack her fist into the popcorn now, I thought. *Yeah, not gonna happen.*

Speaking of Heather, I scanned the bleachers, but saw no sign of her. "Hey, you too good to sit with your buds?" Johnny asked, walking by on his way to the water bottles.

"No, John-boy, I just needed some privacy," I said. "It's a Choctaw thing. We're quiet people, you know."

"Uh-huh," Johnny said, "unless you're awake. But maybe I can help you."

"Help me what?"

"She's sitting in the top row, behind us. Surrounded by her group of Giggle Girls."

My first impulse was to jerk my head around, but I caught myself.

"How'd you know I was looking for her?"

"It's a Cherokee thing," Johnny said. "We read minds."

"Uh-huh. Except when you're awake."

He laughed and took a seat beside me.

"I thought she'd be banned from the games, for a while at least," I said. "For fighting with Faye and wrestling with the cops."

"Wouldn't surprise me if she snuck in," Johnny said.

"I'm sure Faye has already caught sight of her," I said. "But Faye looks happy where she is."

"Have you seen the security guards?" Johnny asked.

"No. Why?"

"You know they always have two at the games. They're big fans. They love coming."

"I see one," I said, pointing to the door leading to the concession stand.

"Promise me you won't look if I tell you where the other one is?"

"Are you joking, Johnny?" I asked.

"Nope, not joking."

"Hoke then, I promise."

"Lloyd's dad is sitting on the far end of the gym, four rows up, near the outside door. A security guard is right next to him. They entered through that door, almost like he's a criminal in leg-irons."

"Lloyd seems hoke," I said. "Is his mother here?"

"She's sitting behind his dad. Pretty strange, if you ask me."

The horn sounded, ending the third quarter and bringing us back to reality. Coach Robison substituted second and third teamers for the remainder of the game. The Tigers made a slight comeback, but came no closer than twelve points.

Final: Panthers 64–Tigers 47.

"No pizza tonight, boys," Coach Robison announced in the dressing room. "Not on a school night. Go home and get some rest. Next game's not till Friday."

We made our way to the parking lot, and Lloyd caught up with Johnny and me. "Can you guys give me a ride home?" he asked.

"Sure thing," Johnny said. "You don't have to ask."

Lloyd didn't reply, but we knew he had something to say. He waited till we climbed in the car and the doors were closed.

"I'm still cool with my old friends," he said. "But I can't talk about Dad. Not with them.

Their parents know mine, and the gossip would be all over town."

"Hey, we're with you, Lloyd," I said. "Johnny was my only friend when it came to Dad. For the longest time."

"They oughta have a group called DAA," Johnny said. "Kinda like AA, Alcoholics Anonymous."

"Hoke, I'm game."

"Yeah, let's hear it," said Lloyd.

"DAA?" said Johnny. "How about: Dad's An Alcoholic?"

"Hoke, so that's what we're doing tonight," Lloyd said. "We're having our first DAA meeting."

We rode in silence till we turned down Lloyd's street.

"I'm scared," said Lloyd. "Dad's moving around the house, banging walls with his fist. He yanked a picture down last night and smashed it, sent glass flying everywhere."

"How's your mom?" I asked.

"She's mostly staying away, coming up with every excuse she can think of. Looks like she's gone," he said as we approached his house. "No car in the driveway."

"Lloyd," I said, "it's time. Trust me, you'll be glad you did."

Johnny understood. He drove by Lloyd's house and headed to mine.

"So I'm spending the night underground," said Lloyd. "Kinda what I was hoping for."

CHAPTER 7

Alone in a Crowd

"You want some company?" I asked Lloyd as I pulled the door over our heads.

"Sure, as long as you don't spend the night. I need some time alone."

Johnny nudged me in the ribs. I knew where he was going. "Yeah," Johnny said, "kid members of Dad's An Alcoholic need that alone time. It's hard to be sad and depressed when you're surrounded by friends!"

"Hey, shut up!" Lloyd said, but he was already laughing.

"So what's up with Heather?" I asked. "She was at the game."

"Oh, you won't believe this," Lloyd said. "She is allowed back at school, allowed to attend the games, but only if she agrees to staying after school an hour a day. For a month!"

"Like detention hall?" I asked.

"A little more than that. She has agreed to be tutored. So she has to do her homework and actually learn something."

"In school?" Johnny said. "She's trying to learn in school? Who came up with that idea?"

"Probably the counselor. Who knows?"

"And who's gonna be her tutor? Man, that's one job I wouldn't want," Johnny said. "You'd have to wear a bulletproof vest."

"Not necessary," said a voice from above. "We had our first session today."

"I'm not believing this," I said, pulling the door aside. There she stood, Mystery Lady Faye.

"So you are Heather's tutor?" Johnny asked.

"That is correct."

"Lloyd, did you know about this?" I asked. Lloyd just shrugged.

"Ahem," Faye said, clearing her throat. "I brought a bucket of chicken and a bag of fries. Anybody hungry?"

"Mystery Lady comes through again!" said Johnny, helping Faye into the hole.

Lloyd pulled his shirt over his head and stammered. "So much for privacy."

Suddenly the patio light came on. "You guys better not be drinking down there!" Dad yelled, stepping out the back door.

"Dad, you know better than that."

"Oh. Hoke, but just in case you're thirsty," he said, "I brought the ice chest. Root beer, grape soda, Doctor my Pepper."

Dad left the ice chest under the tree. "Be safe and be nice to each other," he said, waving goodbye. He turned off the light, and I'm sure he and Mom had a good laugh.

We grabbed chicken legs and thighs and wings and chewed and chomped. After my third swig of root beer, I had to ask.

"So what's up with this tutoring?"

"There was a note on the bulletin board in the library," Faye said. "It asked for a volunteer tutor for a month, an hour after school every day. You had to have a good grade point average."

"And you're doing this for free?" Johnny asked.

"No. They offered free tickets to all sporting events and school performances, plays, and concerts. So I jumped at it."

"And you knew you'd be tutoring Heather?" I asked.

"No way she knew that, right Faye?" Lloyd asked.

"Let's just say I was a little taken aback."

"Man, I wish I had a movie of that first session," Johnny said. "How'd it go?"

"Weird at first," Faye said. "The counselor was waiting in the library with Heather. They were sitting at a table by the window."

"Heather didn't know you were her tutor, did she?" asked Lloyd.

"Nope. It was a big surprise for us both."

Faye took a bite of a crispy chicken wing and kept us waiting.

"You're gonna make us ask, aren't you?" I said.

"Ask what?"

"What happened?" we all shouted in unison.

"Wasn't pretty," Faye said. "Since I'm new at school, the counselor didn't recognize me. I saw Heather before she saw me, so I walked over to the table. They were looking out the window. I was my usual shy self. I quietly sat down."

"Uh-oh," I said.

"Heather turned around and did her screeching thing, so loud everybody in the library heard her. The librarian came running from around the desk. Kids dropped their books and stared."

"What did she say?"

"'Get out of here before I rip your hair out!' That's the one I remember."

"Did you leave?" asked Lloyd.

"No, I did not. I was hired to tutor a student in need. And that is what I did. The counselor told Heather that if she didn't control herself, she would be transferred to another school."

"I know what that means," Johnny said.

"We all do," Lloyd added. "Troubled youth campus. First stop on your way to jail."

"When she calmed down, I told her this wasn't easy for me either. She laughed when I told her I had no idea she was the girl I'd be tutoring."

"I can just hear her now," Johnny said. "Something like, 'You'd be wetting your diaper if you knew you had to put up with me, little Fayby baby.' Am I close?"

"Not bad," said Faye. "You'd make a pretty-good Heather."

"But you survived, sounds like," I said.

"Yes, and believe it or not, I don't think she'll be giving me a hard time in the hallways."

"So you connected," said Lloyd. "Wow. How did you do it?"

"The counselor did me a big favor. I started out with a simple writing lesson. I had Heather write a short paragraph about the coolest thing she ever saw at school."

"You were asking for trouble, did you know that?" Lloyd asked.

"Yes, but it seemed better than avoiding it. So Heather wrote about yanking my hair in the library and how cool she felt doing it. I thought she might, so I was ready."

"What did you do?" Lloyd asked.

"Nothing. I read it and glanced up at her, with a hint of a smile. But when the counselor read it, she was mad. She slapped the paper on the table and told Heather to apologize to me.

"So I gave Heather this little head bob, rolling my eyes at the counselor. At first I thought Heather was gonna sock me. Then she realized I was making fun of the counselor, not her. Heather loved it."

"'Oh, I'm so sorry to hurt your little feelings,' Heather said. That was her apology to me. We both had to laugh. Heather and me, not the counselor. So then the counselor left us alone. She just said, 'Let me know if she gives you any trouble.'"

"Sounds like you didn't impress the counselor," Johnny said.

"I spoke to her later. She's cool. Heather rewrote her paper, and she's making a story out of it."

"What was her favorite time in school?" Lloyd asked.

"Heather's favorite time in school? She wrote half a page about how she watched you work hard every day till you finally became a basketball star. That's what her story is about, Lloyd."

"Yeah! Panthers, Panthers! Go! Go! Go!" Johnny and I cheered so loud, Dad turned on the patio light.

"Any more of that and I'm turning on the water sprinkler!" he hollered.

"Dad, we don't have a water sprinkler," I reminded him.

He didn't answer, just flipped off the light. Dad was so cool. I laughed and said, "What am I gonna do with a dad like that?"

"Count your lucky stars," Lloyd said.

I slapped him on the shoulder. "Hey, Lloyd, you're surrounded by friends, don't forget it."

Two minutes later, Lloyd needed us more than ever. The trouble started with a blaring car horn, loud enough to wake up the whole neighborhood. The noise came from our driveway, but I knew it wasn't Dad. Whoever was doing it kept their hand on the horn without stopping.

BEEEEEEEEP!

"That's my dad," said Lloyd, shouting over the screaming horn. "That's his truck horn. It has to be him!"

CHAPTER 8

Underground Meeting of the Minds

Lights came on up and down the street. Johnny stood up and flung the door aside. I looked at Faye, and we both had the same thought.

Lloyd is in danger.

"Do something," she said, gripping my hand. "Now!"

Lloyd was already climbing out of the hole. I grabbed his pants leg and pulled him back. He plopped down hard against the dirt wall.

"Lloyd, wait. Just a minute. Please," I said. I stood up and leaned close to Johnny's ear. "Hey, we gotta close the door. *Now!* Lloyd's dad can't know where he is. He can't know about our hiding place."

"You're right," Johnny said. "Time for us to disappear." He sat down with his back against the wall and slid the door over our heads.

"You don't understand my dad," Lloyd said. He tried standing up, but I held him by the shoulders.

"Lloyd," I whispered, "there's no time for you to freak out. Leave that to the grown-ups. We're here for you, and you're safe. As long as your dad doesn't know where you are."

Lloyd was shaking. I tugged on him till he sat down.

"My dad was the same way. Think about it. That's why the hole is here in the first place. I had to get away from him. He was breaking things, throwing stuff all over the house."

He buried his face in his hands. "Does it ever end?"

"Yes, and my dad and Coach Robison will do everything they can to help."

"They can't come to my house. They can't be there when I really need them."

Johnny and I just looked at each other. We knew he was right.

Faye had been silent from the time Mr. Blanton arrived. She finally spoke, and her voice seemed to calm the air.

"Hey Bobby," she said, "how about you and Lloyd take me and Heather on a double date? Maybe take in a movie, have a hamburger at the old place you boys keep talking about. I'm new in town, you know. I'd like to know the history of the place."

I looked at Faye. I shrugged my shoulders and opened my palms to her, as if to say, *Are you totally crazy or have you been sleeping for the past five minutes?*

"Nice going, Faye," Johnny said. "Way to make a Cherokee feel unwanted and out of place."

I gave Johnny my best *are you crazy too* look.

What happened next let me know I was without a doubt the *only* sane person in the underground hole in my backyard—the hole I dug to get away from my dad who drank too much. Yeah. The teenager who lived all summer in a hole in his backyard—he's the sane one!

So what happened next, you're wanting to know?

Lloyd started laughing. I didn't want to stop him, so I yanked my shirt off and stuffed it in the pipe. Soon we were all laughing. We laughed and slapped each other on the shoulders, even Faye! We stopped laughing and caught our breath, but that didn't last long.

"We better be quiet," I whisper-laughed. "We'll wake up Coach Robison."

"Yeah, and he'll be over here in a flash, convinced his boys are drinking!" said Johnny.

"No joking about drinking! You can't go there," Lloyd said, but by this time we were all laughing so hard we banged our heads against the dirt wall.

"I like your idea about the date," Lloyd said. "Johnny, can I borrow your phone? I'll give Heather a call, and she can meet us here. Faye, if we keep the lights off so she can't see your hair, you'll be safe."

"Are you sure you're not just a little bit Choctaw, Faye?" I asked. "Only a Choctaw would know how to do what you just did."

"Thank you, Faye," Lloyd said. "I needed that. Bad."

"Needed what?" asked Faye. "We still need to decide what movie we're going to see. This is exciting! My first double date ever, and it all started in a hole in the ground."

Hoke, Johnny, there's your setup. Johnny was the best improv comedian in the group. He didn't let me down.

"Just don't go to any John Wayne movies," he said. "You don't want Faye to know what savages we really are, Bobby."

"Speak for yourself, Cherokee Johnny!" I answered.

"While you guys argue about the movie, I'm going to see Heather," Lloyd said, standing and *almost* lifting the door.

We all shut up and pulled him to his seat.

"Over the top?" he asked. "I'm just trying to be funny like you guys. And gals," he said, nodding to Faye.

She smiled and nodded back.

We sat for the longest time without saying anything. I pulled my shirt from the pipe and looked through the hole to the patio. Nothing there. No lights on in the house. And no loud horn blowing.

"Lloyd, your dad must be gone. No lights on in the house. Dad probably had a talk with him in the driveway."

"Man, what am I gonna do now?"

The question hung over us like a cloud.

"Keep working to the good," I said. "Come to class every day, and play hard, clean basketball. And don't let your temper get the best of you. Lloyd, you're the leader now. Of the Blanton household. Your dad may never admit it, but you have to think like a leader."

Lloyd sighed, and we heard the tough smile in his voice.

"I sure have three good friends to learn from," he said. "And yes, I'm including you, Faye. I know you were only half joking about the date. Let's make it happen."

And so ended the craziest night of the year.

Or so we thought.

CHAPTER 9

A Dad Who's Proud?

I'm sure Mr. Blanton drove home. He didn't hear all the racket we were making in our hideaway room, so Lloyd was safe. For now.

Johnny drove home, and Faye walked through the backyard gate, on the way to her upstairs bedroom in her parents' house next door.

She blinked her lights on and off a few times, so I knew she was thinking of me. I waited on the patio till I saw her lights turn off for the final time, and I knew she would soon be asleep in her own room. I tiptoed through the back door, and in less than five minutes was sound asleep myself.

Sometime after midnight, Lloyd's dad called the house. I knew it had to be him by Dad's response. Dad got out of bed and turned the light on in the living room, so I knew this was something serious. I could only hear Dad's side of the conversation.

"Calm yourself down. Wherever he is, I'm sure he's safe."

"No, I don't know where he is."

"Gimme a minute, I'll ask Bobby."

Of course he didn't ask me anything. He was hoping I was asleep, though he had to know I'd never sleep through this.

"Bobby says Lloyd caught a ride home. Are you sure he's not spending the night with friends?"

"No, it won't do you any good to come over here. I told you Lloyd is not here."

"Now Blanton, I really don't think you should drive. You know what will happen if you get another DWI."

"I'm just trying to help. No, of course I'm not gonna call the police. I am on your side, whether you know it or not."

Of all the lies Dad was feeding Mr. Blanton, he just said the most important truth of the night.

I am on your side, whether you know it or not.

"No, I am not telling you not to drink. I am only saying you are in no condition to drive. And if you take a deep breath and stop screaming, you'll know I'm right."

Dad was getting brave now. Maybe it was working.

"How about this. If you go to bed and get some sleep, I'll call you tomorrow morning. I'll help you find Lloyd."

"Fine. Good night and sleep well."

But the evening was just beginning. Fifteen minutes later, Mr. Blanton showed up at the front door. At least he was smart enough to call a cab. I threw my clothes on and stopped Dad as he went to answer the doorbell.

"Dad," I whispered, "I'm going to be with Lloyd. And don't worry. We're staying underground, no matter what happens."

"Smart move, son. Now hurry up. We'll be sitting on the patio. I'm letting your mom sleep. Somebody needs to around here."

I knocked softly on the door. "Lloyd, it's me. I'm coming in." I pulled the door aside and slid home, closing the door behind me.

"What's going on?" Lloyd asked. "It's past your bedtime."

"Yeah, and I'm hoping you keep up with the jokes. But keep quiet, whatever you do."

"Oh no. It's Dad, isn't it?"

"Yes. He called my dad a little while ago looking for you. Dad couldn't talk him out of it."

"He drove over here?"

"No, and this is the cool part, Lloyd. Your dad took a taxi. He knew he was too drunk to drive."

"Wow. That's never happened before."

I was about to answer him when we heard the patio door slide open. "I've got a little space heater out here," Dad said. "I'll plug it in and make us some coffee. Gimme just a minute."

I looked through the pipe hole and saw Mr. Blanton taking a seat. He blew a breath of air and watched the cold cloud rise from his mouth.

I touched my fingertip to my lips, letting Lloyd know we had to be very quiet. I pointed to the pipe, to let him know I was leaving it open. He touched his ears and gave me a thumbs-up, which meant, *Oh yes. So we can hear everything they say.*

We crouched on our knees, with our ears turned close to the pipe. Mr. Blanton spoke first.

"I'm worried about my son. My wife is out of her mind."

"Is she afraid for Lloyd?" Dad asked.

"Naw, nothing like that. That's how crazy she is. I don't know what to do with her. She don't even care if Lloyd shows up or not. All she wants to do is 'get some sleep and we'll find him in the morning.' That's what she keeps saying. But I ain't sleeping till I get ahold of that boy. He can't just run around all night long. No telling what he and his buddies are up to!"

Dad listened without saying a word, sipping his coffee and nodding in agreement. When Mr. Blanton paused and reached for his coffee, Dad spoke.

"I can pretty much guarantee that Lloyd's not partying with his teammates," he said, slapping Mr. Blanton on the knee. "Not like you and I would have done, anyway."

"You got that right," Mr. Blanton said, tossing his coffee down with one gulp, then spitting it on the ground. "Oh yeah, we knew how to party."

He shook his head and smiled, bringing back the memories.

"See what I mean, Lloyd," I whispered. "You and I have a lot in common."

"Yeah," he answered, "we're both members of DAA. Dad's An Alcoholic."

I had to cover my mouth to keep from laughing out loud. I'd forgotten our new version of the Boys Club. "This is maybe our most important meeting yet," I said.

"If you think back on all we did, it's a wonder we're still alive," Dad said.

"If you call this living!" Mr. Blanton said.

More silence as Dad let that thought slip in. He took another sip of coffee. "At least you don't have to worry about Lloyd doing what Bobby did," he finally said.

"And what's that?"

"Bobby hid out somewhere all summer long. I didn't know where he was. You remember me talking about it at the bar."

"Wasn't he with your wife? Didn't she leave?"

"Yeah, she left. But Bobby didn't go with her."

"Man, that musta been tough."

"I was too drunk to worry about Bobby," Dad said, and this must have hurt him to say. He knew I was listening. But he had a good reason for saying it. He wanted Mr. Blanton to get a glimpse of what life was like for Lloyd. "You must care a lot about your son, to come looking for him in the middle of the night."

I glanced at Lloyd. I couldn't see his face, but I could imagine what he looked like, jaw dropped and fighting away the tears.

"I'm sure he don't know it," Mr. Blanton said, "but I do care for that boy. Did you see that last basketball game? Me and his momma can't stop talking about him."

"We both have boys to be proud of," Dad said.

Lloyd turned away from the pipe and flopped against the wall. "That can't be my dad," he said quietly, not even trying to hide the tears. "If I wasn't hiding out in this hole, he'd be whipping me with his belt. Or shoving me around the house."

I had to ask. "Has he ever hit you with his fist, Lloyd?"

As soon as the words left my mouth, I wished I hadn't said it. But I had to know, and to my surprise, Lloyd answered right away.

"He's never busted my jaw, if that's what you mean. Yeah, he's hit me a few times. How'd you think I got so good at running up and down the court?"

I couldn't believe Lloyd was making a joke now, after midnight and hiding in a hole to get away from his dad. But, as I knew, that's sometimes the only way to get by from day to day. You cry in private and joke when other people are around.

"But he hasn't hit me since he promised Coach Robison he wouldn't," Lloyd said.

I tapped my mouth with my finger, for silence, and pointed to the pipe. We both leaned close to listen, and I looked through the hole. Lloyd's dad was standing up and backing away from the table.

This can't be good.

"I don't know about that," he said. "I've come too far to quit now. I'm bringing my boy home tonight," he said.

"So how about I drive you home?" Dad said. "You don't have to call a taxi."

"It's a school night! My boy is out after midnight! No way I'm going home and sleeping."

Talk about perfect timing. At first I was distracted by the light coming on in Mom and Dad's bedroom. Then quickly the light flicked off again, and less than a minute later, Dad's phone rang.

Is Mom calling Dad? What's going on?

"Hello," Dad said. "Yes, he is here. You want to talk to him? I'm hoping this is about Lloyd. Sure, here he is. Thanks, Coach."

Mr. Blanton balled up his fists and pressed them against his cheeks, rocking back and forth as he listened to the conversation.

When Dad held the phone to him, he grabbed it.

"You got Lloyd with you! You better have a good reason, and you better tell me now!"

CHAPTER 10

Midnight Express

Mr. Blanton screamed at the top of his voice, shaking the phone hard and waving his fist at it. "I am sick and tired of you telling me what to do! I can call the cops on you, for having my boy out this late at night! Lemme talk to him! Now!"

When he finally stopped yelling to take a breath, Dad eased the phone away from him. "Take it easy," he said. "You've got a right to be mad. Let's get you home now."

Dad opened the door to the house and motioned for Mr. Blanton to follow him inside. As he turned to close the door, Dad stepped outside, for only a moment, and motioned for us to climb out of the hole, pointing around the side of the house. We pulled the door aside and hurried out.

Keeping in the shadows, we ran around the garage side of the house. Mom was waiting for us in the driveway, her car engine running. "Jump in," Mom said. "Both of you! Quick!"

Still not knowing what was going on, we did as we were told. We hopped in the back seat. *In case we need to duck*, I thought.

"Mom, where are we going?"

"We're taking Lloyd home. Coach got a call from your mom, Lloyd. She was afraid for you and asked him to try to find out where you were. He guessed you were here, so he's telling your dad that you are home now."

"Dad's gonna be furious when he finds out where I was," Lloyd said.

"You were playing ball down at the outdoor court, late. And if anybody wants to know why, it's because you were afraid to go home. Coach will be there when we arrive. He's planning on staying around and settling everybody down."

"So Dad's taking Mr. Blanton home?" I asked.

"Yes, Bobby," Mom said. "Your dad and Coach will both stay as long as they need to.

Coach feels like it's time for a serious talk. Lloyd, you have a lot of people looking out for you."

"Thanks. I just wish this could someday be over with."

"You've got one thing going for you, Lloyd," I said.

"What's that?"

"You're a senior. In a few months, you choose. Stay or go."

"Easy choice. The problem is *where*."

As we pulled into Lloyd's driveway, the porch light came on. His mother peered through the curtains, and when she saw it was us, she opened the door.

"Stay down, Bobby," Mom said. Lloyd dashed inside, and Mom met Mrs. Blanton at the door. I couldn't hear what she said, but what she did was pretty cool. She gave Lloyd's mom a huge hug, kissed her on the forehead, and dashed back to the car.

"That kinda seals the friendship, right Mom?"

"You know it, son. Now let's get home before Dad and his friend arrive."

"No problem there," I said. "Knowing Dad, he'll probably drop by the bar for a few beers. Just to seal the friendship."

"Not funny, Bobby. Not funny."

But she was shaking her head and smiling, so it was *kinda* funny, in a Choctaw way.

By the time we arrived home, we were both yawning. "Nothing we can do but wait, Bobby," Mom said. "Let's get some sleep, and I'll stay close to the phone."

"You promise?"

"Yes, Bobby. I'll wake you up with any news."

I climbed into bed, and the next thing I knew, Dad was knocking on my door and hollering. "It's time to get up, it's time to get up, it's time to get up in the morning!"

"I'm on it, Dad!" I shouted. "And I expect a full report over breakfast."

"Might be short. It's a school day, remember?"

Oh yeah. That little detail.

I jumped out of bed and was dressed and ready to go in less than five. Dad was coffeed up, pump-fisted, and ready to talk as I made my way to the kitchen.

"Waffles hoke?" Mom asked, serving me a double-decker plate of waffles and raspberry syrup.

"Looking good, Mom," I said, then turned to Dad. "Whenever you're ready."

"Well, son, I guess you can tell by my upbeat attitude that nobody went to jail. Nobody got punched. Nobody got drunk."

"Wait, Dad. Wasn't Mr. Blanton already drunk?"

"Bobby, you want to talk or listen?"

"Sorry, Dad," I said, smiling. Dad was joking, but he was right. I could tell everything went fine at the Blantons'.

"Lloyd was in bed when we arrived. I'm sure he wasn't asleep, since me and Blanton got there maybe ten minutes after you and Mom drove away. But with Lloyd already in bed, Blanton had nobody to bully and yell at."

"You think he would have yelled at Lloyd? Even with you and Coach Robison there?"

"Bobby, he smashed a chair through Coach's window, and he didn't care who saw him. Yeah, sometimes a bully likes an audience."

"Oh, right," I said. "Like Heather at the basketball games."

"Exactly," Mom said. "Bobby, bullies are alike in one big way. They act like they're king of the hill, in total control. But they are the most insecure people you'll ever meet."

"And most of them grew up being bullied," Dad said, looking at his coffee and showing a sadness in his eyes.

"Hey, Dad," I said, "we're cool now. Mom wasn't talking about you!"

"I know, Bobby, but she could have been."

"Sorry, men," Mom said. "I'll be quiet and let you talk."

We all shared an easy laugh, a good family laugh. I finished my waffles and orange juice, and Dad tossed down his coffee.

"Hoke," he said, "Coach said he wanted you and Lloyd at school early again this morning, so grab your books and we'll talk on the way to school."

"Time sure flies when you're having fun," I said.

As Dad backed out of the driveway, he spoke in a more serious tone. "Bobby," he said, "I wanted to talk to you alone. I'm not trying to keep anything from your mom, but I didn't want to start her day worrying."

"What happened, Dad?"

"We had a good talk, and Mrs. Blanton didn't hold back. She told Blanton how Lloyd was afraid of him, just like she was, when he was drinking. 'We never know what you'll do,' she said. And Blanton listened. He even said 'I'm sorry' a few times."

We were nearing the school, and Dad slowed down. I knew he had something important to tell me. I waited.

"We'll talk more later. I want to tell you something nobody else knows. And please don't say anything to Lloyd about it."

"You can trust me, Dad."

"I know, son. So we were ready to go home, and Blanton stepped out on the patio. I followed him. He was breathing so hard you could see his breath in the cold air. I wanted to say something encouraging, Bobby, but something told me to wait, see what he had to say."

"Did he want to talk to you in private, Dad?" I asked.

"I think he stepped outside just to get away. But he did finally talk, and I'm so glad I was there. He said it hasn't been easy for him. Before

Lloyd started playing basketball, he did what his dad told him to do, but things are different now. Blanton admitted he used to whip Lloyd's butt when he needed it, but now he feels like he's gotta get Coach Robison's approval before he does anything with his own son and he's not happy about that."

"He's still mad at Coach, isn't he Dad?"

"Yes. He said he was doing his best to hold on, but he'd like to bust Coach in the mouth. I'm afraid this isn't over with. Stay close to Lloyd. I'm worried."

"I will, Dad. And thank you for trusting me."

"Have a good day, Bobby, and play well."

CHAPTER 11

Bobby Backtalk

As I stepped into the gym, I saw Lloyd shooting free throws at the far end of the court. Coach Robison was still in his office, but he soon joined us—with a manly smile.

"Morning, boys," he said. "Nice game last night. Well played, both of you. I hope you see how much you're improving, Lloyd."

"Thank you, Coach. Yes, it feels good."

"Now," he said, "I'm not going to ask you to forget about last night. I can't do that, and I won't ask you to either. But let's agree on one thing. We tuck it away for later times, not to be ignored but to be dealt with later. Out in the open someday, just not today. Can we do that?"

"Yes sir, Coach," I said.

"Thank you," Lloyd said with a grateful nod.

"So, let's keep improving that left hand, Lloyd. Start by going hard to your right, then pivot and change hands, driving to your left. Bobby, you guard Lloyd and try to knock the ball away. Steal the ball and drive in for a score."

"I'm on it, Coach," I said.

"Good. Both of you guys get your turn with the ball. Lloyd, you go first." Coach usually returned to his office after giving us the day's drill, but not this morning. He wanted to make sure we worked hard and focused on basketball. I could read his mind. *Gotta focus.*

No drama at school on Tuesday. Nothing abnormal. But sometime in the middle of the night, Dad came knocking at my door.

"Bobby, you wanna do something really weird?" he asked. "I mean totally weird? Wake up, Bobby. Your momma says it's hoke, which means we can go do it. Knowing your momma, we'd get in big trouble otherwise, but she says we can go, so let's do it."

"What are you talking about, Dad?"

"I'm talking about crawling up outta bed, putting on your basketball shorts and T-shirt and shoes and socks, and getting out of here right now!"

"Dad, are you feeling hoke?"

"Bobby, I'll be feeling hoke when you say, 'Yes, sir,' just like little boys are supposed to say when their dad tells 'em what to do. They say, 'Yes, sir,' and then they do it!"

"Yes, sir," I said, in my best little boy's voice.

In two minutes flat I was standing in the living room in my dark-blue Panther-on-the-side shorts and my light-blue Panthers T-shirt, with my basketball shoes on but no socks. I still thought this was some kind of a joke.

"Bobby, you can't play basketball without socks. Didn't Coach Robison teach you anything? You will never get a college basketball scholarship if you can't remember to put your socks on *first*, then your shoes. Now say it with me, Bobby. *Socks first, then my shoes.*"

It had to be close to three o'clock in the morning. I stared at Dad. He rolled his fingers into fists and slapped his arms to his hips, glaring at me the entire time.

This was so far over the top, I decided to play along.

Once again—in my best little boy's voice—I said, "Dad, please give me another chance to repeat it with you. I'll do better, I promise."

"Hoke, son. Last chance. Here we go."

He raised his pointed fingers in front of him, like a symphony conductor, then nodded and pointed at me. We chanted in unison, "Socks first, then my shoes."

"How'd I do, Dad?"

"You did fine, son. Now hurry up and I'll start the truck."

"You're actually going through with this?" No more little boy's voice.

"No back talk, Bobby, unless you want that to be your Choctaw name. Bobby Backtalk?"

"No way, Dad. I'm on it." As I dashed to the bedroom for my socks, I thought, *No Name is a better name than Bobby Backtalk!*

Dad must have been reading my mind. He had a big grin on his face when I returned. "No more No Name. Right, Bobby?"

"Right, Dad," I said. "I'll put my socks on in the truck. Let's go!"

Dad paused at the door, then slowly turned his head around facing me. "What did you say?"

"Oh, I'm sorry, Dad. Of course I meant to say, 'May I please put my socks on in the truck, Dad?'"

"That's better, Bobby. Yes, you may."

I hopped in the truck, Dad started the engine, and Mom waved at us from their bedroom window. I waited till we reached the end of the block before speaking in my real-life Bobby Byington voice.

"I'm enjoying the play, Dad, don't get me wrong. But can we say it's intermission?"

"Yeah, I'm getting a little tired of playing mean man, drunk Daddy. Or even mean man, sober Dad."

"Yeah, I've grown to like the nice guy. So which is real and which is the act?" I asked, then wished I hadn't.

Dad drove without answering for several blocks. He turned down the road to the park and said, "I'm just glad we're able to joke about the mean dad I used to be, Bobby. I think it hurts me more than anybody to remember what I used to be like."

"Dad, Mom came back, and so did I, because we know you're a good guy. And you proved us right."

"Oh, son, how many Mr. Blantons are there in the world that may never hear that?"

"I'm proud of you and Coach for doing all you can to help Lloyd's family."

Dad pulled to the curb by the park and turned to me. "You're proud of us, Bobby?" He smiled and shook his head. "What does an old man say when his son says he's proud of him?"

That needed no answer. I hopped from the truck as Dad reached behind the seat for his basketball.

"Think you can shoot in the dark, son?"

"I don't know, Dad," I said. "It's not easy playing without a few hundred people cheering your every move. What happens when I nail a three-pointer and nobody cares?"

I stepped to the corner of the court as Dad tossed me a long pass. I caught it over my shoulder, took two quick dribbles, and launched a long ball.

Nothing but net! Or more accurately, nothing but chains, as outdoor goals don't have nets.

"Bobby scores a bucket, and Daddy gets the dime," he called out, then slapped his hand over his mouth. "Oops," he said, in a quieter voice.

"Folks in the neighborhood are trying to sleep. I guess we better keep it down."

"Good idea, Dad."

By now the ball had rolled off the court and under a tree. I ran and grabbed it and tossed it to Dad. "Let's see your long ball, old man."

Dad stood in the grass, ten feet from the court. He lowered the basketball almost to his waist and flung it to the rim. Not even close. I caught the ball before it hit the court and dribbled away from the basket. Without looking, I tossed it backward over my shoulder, high and slow, giving Dad time to make the running catch. He did, and also made the lay-up.

"Yo, Dad," I said. "I get the dime, and you get the bucket."

"Way to keep it in the family, Bobby."

We carried on with our father-son foolishness for another twenty minutes or so. I had yet to ask the key question.

What in blazes are we doing here?

CHAPTER 12

Leafy Dad Comes Clean

I knew Dad would tell me when he was ready, and finally the time came. The moon hid behind the clouds and the court was cast in darkness. I tucked the ball under my arm and sat against the tree.

"Yeah, time to take it easy," Dad said, and I could hear his heavy breathing. He joined me, back against the trunk. I waited.

"The memories, the memories," he said in almost a whisper. "There's a lot about drinking that sober people never understand. Even though we all have our drinking buddies, maybe a dozen close friends, we're all very much alone. We try to love our wives, our kids, but nothing works. When the bar closes and we head to the house, we go alone.

"Many times, Bobby, I'd drive down here, to this outdoor playground, and shoot some hoops. All by myself, sometimes too drunk to hit the backboard. Sometimes I'd throw up in the bushes and hope nobody would notice."

"Did Mom know?"

"No, Bobby. She was always asleep when I got home."

I knew Dad wanted to share something with me. I had a feeling that although I was still very much his son, I was also becoming a good friend—to my own dad.

"I'll never forget one night," Dad said. "I drove down here after drinking with Blanton and a tableful of other drunks. You were maybe two years old. I was mad about something somebody said at the bar. Don't ask me what. But whatever it was, it really got under my skin.

"I was driving way too fast and slammed on the brakes. Skidded against the curb. I do remember jumping out and slamming the door. I ran to the court and pounded the ball hard. I tried dribble-driving from one end to the other, but I was too drunk.

"I stumbled and rolled up against a tree. When I tried to get up, I was too dizzy to even stand. I finally flopped on the ground and fell asleep. I didn't wake up till maybe an hour before sunrise. You still with me, Bobby?" Dad asked, glancing my way.

"Sure, Dad. Always."

"That's my Bobby," he said laughing. "Yeah. Well, I hurried home before I realized it was a Saturday and I didn't have to go to work. But I was getting home four hours later than usual, at least. And your mom was up."

"Did she stay up waiting for you?"

"She might have, Bobby. I never asked her. But her eyes were bloodshot and she'd been crying, I could tell that for sure. As soon as I stepped through the door, she stood up to meet me. She'd been waiting in the living room, and she had her robe on."

I buried my face in my palms. This was hard to hear, but easy to imagine—Dad stumbling into the house, and Mom sipping coffee and waiting for him.

"You hoke, Bobby?"

"Yeah, Dad. Please go on," I said, never lifting my face. Dad understood. *Truth hurts but must be told.* He'd said it himself many times in the past year.

"Your mom didn't let me walk in the house like nothing had happened. Not this morning. 'You think I don't know where you've been?' she asked me."

"Wow. Mom said that?"

"Yes, she did, Bobby. And that's just the beginning. 'You've been to the park,' she said, pointing to my shirt. 'You've got leaves all over you. You spent the night in the park. And you wouldn't be out this late by yourself.' She walked past me to the bedroom and shut the door behind her."

"So Mom thought you spent the night at the park with someone else?" I had to ask.

Dad sighed and shook his head. "Yes, son. That's what she still thinks, if she ever remembers that night."

"You never told her the truth?"

"No, Bobby. I didn't want to go there again. We had too many things to fight about without digging up the past."

"But, Dad, things have changed now. You've got to tell her."

Dad wasn't convinced, I could tell. "Let's head to the house, Bobby. We can both use some sleep."

I followed him to the truck and acted cool. No probs. But I had a plan, a good one. When we pulled into the driveway, I didn't wait for Dad to put it in park. Nope. I dashed to the door, leaving it open behind me so Dad could hear everything I said.

I opened the door to their bedroom, which I never did. I flicked on the light and shouted, "Mom, get up! Come on! Dad's got the biggest surprise of the year. He's got a story to tell you. Time to wake up, Mom."

She lifted her face from the pillow and rubbed her eyes.

"Bobby, this better be good," she said. "And if it's your dad's story, why are you waking me up at . . ." She glanced at the bedside alarm clock. "Three thirty a.m.?"

"You're right, Mom. I'll let Dad tell you. Oh, here he is!"

Dad stood behind me with a serious look on his face. "You will pay for this, son," he whispered.

"I think I better hit the sack," I said.

Dad shut the door and flicked the light off. But I'm sure he told her the story of his leafy night at the park, with much more detail than the version he had shared with me.

Good night, I thought, as I fluffed my pillow up and buried my head in it. But before I drifted off to sleep, I had a realization.

Dad knew I would say something to Mom about that night. Maybe that's why we went to the park in the first place. I was his intro man. Yeah. That's me. No more No Name.

Now I'm Bobby Backtalk!

And that was only Wednesday.

CHAPTER 13

Baldy Lady Faye

School-day Wednesday was a day to remember.

Faye met me on the sidewalk outside the gym, and something about her was different. When she saw me scrunching up my face in a question, she flipped her hair.

"Do you like it, Bobby?" she asked.

"Uh, yeah. I guess so. What did you do?"

"I fluffed it up a little and gave it a few blonde streaks. What do you think?"

Hoke. That was weird enough, for Faye to even care what her hair looked like. But what she did next made me wonder if this was my next-door neighbor or some imposter.

Faye, Mystery Lady Faye, shy neighbor Faye, planted her chin on her left shoulder and turned around so slowly she looked like a model on a reality show.

"Well," I stammered, "I don't know what to say. You mind telling me why you did that?"

"That's for me to know and you to find out," she said, flipping her hair one final time as we entered the hallway. "See you later. If you're lucky!"

I laughed so loud everybody turned to stare at me. "Sorry," I said, slapping my hands over my mouth. I didn't have long to wait for the answer to my question.

An hour later, as we stood in the hallway between classes, Faye told me the whole story.

"Heather and I had an early morning tutoring session," she said, "and I planned a special surprise for her. If we're going to really get along, we needed a breakthrough moment."

"A breakthrough moment? With Heather that sounds like broken bones."

"That was before. Things are different now. Heather still screeches at me in the library, but she's much quieter than before. And when she yanks my hair, she does it playfully."

"I bet she loved your new hairdo," I said.

"Oh yes. I knew she would. I also knew she would yank it extra hard, since my hair looks better than hers!"

"And you wanted her to yank hard?"

"Yes, Bobby," Faye said quietly. "But I have a secret." She glanced up and down the hallway, then placed her fingers to her lips. "Shhh," she whispered.

I'm glad she warned me, or else I would have hollered loud enough to shake the building. Faye lifted her hair from her head and handed it to me. My jaw dropped as I stared at Faye's bald, pink head, without a single hair on it.

"Ohhh, Faye. What happened to you?"

Faye covered her mouth with her fist and laughed, rocking back and forth against the wall. "It's hoke, Bobby. Go ahead and touch my bald head. You know you want to."

Of course I didn't want to, but when she leaned over and nudged me in the chest, I had to touch it. It felt weird and rubbery!

"Hoke, Faye, time for some truth telling," I said.

"So you think you're the only one who can fool the world? Huh, Bobby? You with your underground hole that you lived in for a summer."

I shrugged my shoulders and didn't know what to say.

"Bug-eyed Bobby, maybe that's your new name," Faye said, still laughing. "Hoke, so I bought a swimmer's head cap and colored it with makeup to match my skin. Then I found this wig in a beauty salon—almost my hair color, except for the blonde streaks. I cut my hair shorter than usual, tucked it under the cap, put on the wig, and pranced my way to school.

"When you didn't guess it was a wig this morning, I knew I would fool Heather. And man, did I fool Heather!"

"And you're still alive to tell about it," I said, shaking my head. "That's what surprises me."

"You should have seen her in the library. I arrived early for our session, and when she saw my hairdo, she practically ran across the floor, grabbed my hair, and screeched, 'You think you're the pretty girl now? Let's see if you like how pretty feels!'

"She yanked on my hair so hard she almost fell over backwards. Everyone in the library was watching, and when they saw her holding my hair in her hand, they all started screaming! It was a once-in-a-lifetime happening, Bobby! You should have been there!"

"And then?" I asked, still feeling like Bobby Bug-Eyed.

"The librarian hurried over, and when she saw me, and Heather, and my hair, and my bald head, she grabbed a chair to keep from falling. 'Should I call someone?' she asked.

"I took my wig from Heather, very matter-of-factly. 'No, everything is fine,' I told her. 'I just hope my hair grows back.' I turned to Heather and said, 'Are you ready for some tutoring?'

"Heather took her seat and gave me the biggest smile I've ever seen on her face. 'For my first lesson,' she said, 'I want to know exactly how you did that. I want to borrow that trick. Not for school, but for a nasty stepmother who grabs my hair.'"

"Faye," I said, "I'm not saying you're the smartest girl I've ever met. And I'm not saying you're the craziest. No need to say it."

"Will you kiss me and make it all better?"

In the hallway, without even looking around to see if anybody was watching, I planted a sweet kiss on Mystery Lady Faye's lips. A quick kiss, since we were already late for class.

CHAPTER 14

Elbow to the Face

Then came Friday.

"Toughest team we've faced all year," Coach Robison said as we prepared to take the court. "But you men have overcome so much in your lives, on and off the court. I have faith in you. Have faith in yourselves."

Lloyd and I were both on the starting five now, along with Jimmy, Johnny, and Darrell.

Panthers, Panthers! Go! Go! Go!

Johnny lost the opening tip, and we soon learned Coach was right. These guys were tough. A quick pass to the corner, a man cut to the basket and faked a short bank shot. Darrell's feet left the floor to block the shot, his man ducked under him, scored the basket, and was fouled. Ten seconds into the game and we were down by three.

Didn't get much better. They were ready for everything we tried. When Lloyd drove hard to his right, then spun for the pass to the free-throw line, my man dropped off and intercepted the pass.

They sped downcourt, and I was facing a three-on-one fast break. I stopped the dribbler on the baseline and he lobbed it over my head for a lay-up.

Down by 5.

This was our final pre-district game, against a larger school near McAlester. And they were tall, fast, and skilled. They played a double-post offense, with one post man on the free-throw line and the other under the basket. Their toughest under-the-bucket player rotated from one baseline to the other.

With the score Eagles 9–Panthers 2, Coach called our first time-out. He did everything he could to settle us down. "They play *city* ball," he said. "They will shove and push—more than you men have seen. They'll foul hard and complain when the refs start calling it. So be ready.

"We need to get some points on the board. We play best at full speed, so don't slow it up. But if they're back on defense, run your plays. Drive and kick it out for the jump shot. And Bobby, don't be afraid to launch some threes. Even if you miss, those long bounces give us a better chance at the rebound. Now, I want everyone's attention."

Coach paused, waiting for that powerful moment when we moved to the same heartbeat. "Never doubt yourselves," he said. "You are skilled and intelligent basketball players. Do your best."

We leaned in and offered our hands.

"Yeah!" we shouted, then took the court.

Following Coach's advice, we felt a new determination. And we also noticed a touch of attitude from our opponents. Lloyd dribbled across midcourt and tossed me the ball near the sideline. I fired a three-pointer and scored. The crowd now had something to cheer about. Eagles 9–Panthers 5.

But the Eagles let me know right away they were not impressed. I played tight defense on my man as he set up their play with a slow dribble. He threw a quick pass to a post man and cut to the basket. I stayed tight on him, and he didn't like it.

He also didn't like that I'd scored on him. He gave me a slight push, and when that didn't free him, he gave me an elbow to the jaw. Coach Robison saw it, but the refs let it go. He caught a quick pass and scored. Eagles 11–Panthers 5.

Coach called a time-out and motioned for both referees to join him on the sideline. He spoke respectfully, but his message was clear.

"You missed a deliberate foul, an elbow to the face of my player right after he hit the three-pointer. Did you not see it?"

Both men shook their heads, and the lead ref said, "We call it as we see it, Coach, and we don't want anyone to get hurt."

Coach Robison gave them each a strong look and turned to the bench. "Are you hoke, Bobby?" he asked.

"Yes, I'm fine."

"Need a break?"

"No, sir, I'd like to play."

"Good, I was hoping so. Gather around," he said. "Men, I called a time-out to let the refs know I'm not happy with the dirty play. And also to let you all know that I will not tolerate any retaliation. We play clean and hard, is that understood?"

"Yes, sir!" we said, as the buzzer sounded and we took to the court.

I never expected what happened next.

As if to make a point, the entire Eagles team picked up the attitude. When Lloyd began his dribble-drive, the man guarding him made a swipe at the ball. As Lloyd drove by him, he stuck out his leg and tripped him. Lloyd fell hard to the floor.

The referee blew his whistle and called a non-shooting foul. The Panthers crowd grew silent. I ran to Lloyd, who was rolling on the floor in pain, trying to get up.

Out of the corner of my eye, I saw his dad slowly stand. The security guard was no longer sitting by him.

Not good, I thought. Mr. Blanton pushed his way through the crowd, stepping down from the bleachers to courtside. He glared at the referee nearest the play. Even from across the gym, I could see the anger in his face, the tension in his muscles. His fists were clenched. I was reminded of my dad, a teenager lying on the sidewalk in front of the courthouse. Struck by his father.

Please, no. Lloyd does not need this.

Dad was watching Mr. Blanton too. He caught him before he stepped on the court, taking him by the shoulder in a firm but friendly way. I don't know what Dad said to him, but as Lloyd was carried off the court and to the dressing room, his dad followed.

My dad walked between Mr. Blanton and the referees, preventing any real trouble.

CHAPTER 15

Win One for Lloyd

The head referee blew his whistle and waved his arms as he dashed to the sideline.

"Personal foul on number 32 of the Eagles, and a technical foul also," he said, raising his hands high and making the T sign. He motioned for the coaches to join him in front of the scorer's table.

"Coach," he said, addressing the Eagles' coach, "you need to warn your team that any more conduct like this and we'll send players to the locker room."

"I think we have already reached that point," Coach Robison said. "He deliberately tripped my player, and he is out for the remainder of the game, maybe longer. He is hurt."

"Officials' time-out!" shouted the head referee.

The referees waved the coaches away and huddled together for a moment of private conversation.

When they emerged from their discussion, the head referee stepped to center court. A strange hush floated over the gym. In a voice loud enough for all to hear, he announced, "Number thirty-two of the Eagles is expelled from the game and will be removed from the court. The Panthers will shoot two shots for the technical foul and take the ball out of bounds."

The home crowd stood up and clapped, and the cheerleaders even tried to fire them up with "Panthers, Panthers! Go! Go! Go!"

Didn't happen. What rose from the wooden bleachers was a quieter cheering and clapping. A serious cloud of worry hung in the air.

How is Lloyd?

"Jimmy, you knock down the free throws," Coach said. "Bart, take Lloyd's place and let Bobby bring the ball downcourt. They're not gonna want to foul, so let's throw the ball inside.

Jimmy, Darrell, we need you two to be monsters around the basket. Go up hard and fight for every rebound. Let's cut into that lead, men!"

"Yeah!" we shouted.

"Let's win this game for Lloyd," I said in a soft voice.

Coach Robison stepped back and stared at me like he was seeing me for the first time. His eyebrows rose and he nodded, giving me a look of pure pride.

"I like that," Coach said. "What do you say, Panthers? Gimme your hands again. On three, let's shout—for everyone in the gym to hear— *win this one for Lloyd!*"

"One. Two. Three. *Win this one for Lloyd!*"

Now the crowd picked up the cheers. The gym was rocking with excitement, and for the first time, we believed we could actually win this game.

Jimmy did hit both free throws to cut the lead to 11–7.

We quickly learned who was their go-to guy when they needed a bucket. Danny Mack, the big man for the Eagles, and he was not a typical high school post player. He was not long and lean like Cherokee Johnny, who stood six foot two. He was taller than Johnny by several inches—six foot five, I'm guessing.

He had good spring in his legs. We all saw that he dunked his lay-ups during warm-ups. He had a powerful chest and muscled-up arms for pushing his way to the basket or clearing space for a rebound.

"It's going inside," Coach Robison hollered.

Johnny nodded. He stepped in front of Danny so the pass was lobbed over his head. Darrell left his man, and when Danny grabbed the ball and turned to shoot, Darrell swatted it away.

Danny didn't like that. He threw his hands in the air and looked to the ref. "What? No foul?" he shouted.

While he argued with the referee, Bart and I played pitch and catch, fast-breaking downcourt. I stopped at the top of the circle and took one dribble to ease into my jump shot. The lone Eagle back for the break stopped and waved a hand in my face.

I never intended to shoot a three. This was Bart's basket. My dime and Bart's lay-up. I threw him a nice bounce pass and he banked it in.

Eagles 11–Panthers 9.

Now the crowd was into it. Big time. And for once the cheerleaders added a new line.

Panthers, Panthers! Go! Go! Go!

Eagles fly but way too slow!

The Eagles' coach called a time-out. Coach Robison had a smile on his face, but he shook his head in the direction of the cheerleaders.

"If they weren't upset before, they will be now!" he said. "Hoke, men, good hustle. And I hope you learned something about complaining to the refs when the ball is in play. If anyone complains, it will be me. That's my job, understand?"

"Yes, sir!"

"Good. I expect them to keep going to the post. Danny is strong, and he won't lose the ball like that again. Darrell, slide back and you and Johnny double-team him the next few times downcourt. Let's see if he'll give up the ball."

"Let's go!" shouted the lead referee, and the Eagles threw the ball in to begin play.

Coach guessed right. The Eagles' plan was to get the ball to Danny. My man threw a pass to the corner, and Danny muscled his way in front of Johnny. He caught the ball less than ten feet from the basket and took two dribbles, backing into Johnny. Darrell left his man for the double-team, but Danny was too quick.

Easy bank shot. Eagles 13–Panthers 9.

As we hurried down on offense, Coach called Darrell over. "Don't be afraid to leave your man," he said. "We need to see if he'll give up the ball. Something tells me he won't."

Now that Danny had quieted the crowd for a moment—and now that Lloyd's injury seemed a thing of the past to the Eagles—that attitude returned. Johnny was the next victim.

I threw the ball to Bart in the corner, expecting a return pass for another three-pointer. Instead, he lobbed it into Johnny. Danny backed off, daring him to shoot. Johnny was only eight feet from the basket, an easy bank shot.

As he rose to release the ball, Danny stayed on his feet. Instead of trying to block the shot, he put his hand on Johnny's chest and shoved him hard. The shot flew over the basket, and Johnny rolled to the floor.

I will never forget what Johnny did next. My mind flew back to that day on the playground when Jimmy and Darrell and Bart showed up—

to challenge us and give us a hard time. Jimmy had elbowed Johnny in the jaw, a deliberate and dirty move. As the blood dripped to the concrete court, Johnny had said, "I thought you came to play basketball." That day, Johnny and I earned the respect of our future teammates by *not* fighting.

Just like that first day on the playground, Johnny didn't let it bother him. He leapt to his feet. Even as the crowd booed and waved their arms at the dirty foul, Johnny turned and waved to our fans with a smile on his face.

I hope his dad is watching this.

CHAPTER 16

Clean, Hard Basketball

"Stay seated, men," Coach Robison said, moving quickly up and down the bench. "I know you're upset. So am I, but let's give the referees a chance. That's what they're here for."

He then turned and faced the court, folding his arms and staring at the refs.

"You're gone!" shouted the lead referee, pointing to Danny and moving to the scorer's table. "Technical foul, number fifteen of the Eagles," he said, making the T sign for the second time in less than five minutes. "Shooting foul, also number fifteen."

Approaching the Eagles' bench, he said, "Coach, take number fifteen to the dressing room and see that he does not return to the gym tonight. He is not to sit in the stands or be anywhere in the gym, is that understood?"

"Yes. I'll take care of it." The coach turned to his assistant and spoke briefly, then had a serious but short talk with Danny as he walked him off the court.

The referee blew his whistle and called an officials' time-out. He spoke to the other refs, and his assistant came to our bench. "We need to settle down and play," he said. "I have been informed that any more violent episodes and players will be suspended for several games, not just tonight. Is that clear?"

"We'd like nothing better than to play a clean, hard game," Coach said.

"Good. That's what we want to see."

We gathered around Coach Robison, waiting for instructions. Some of the crowd had sat back down, but many of our fans were still booing and waving their disapproval at the Eagles' bench.

"Hold on a minute," Coach said. He stepped on the court, turning his back to us and facing the crowd. He lifted his arms, palms up, to the ceiling, then motioned for everyone to have a seat.

The entire crowd—every man, woman, and child—showed their respect for Coach Robison. A sweet hush settled over the gym as everyone took their seats.

"Wow," Jimmy said. "I have never seen anything like that before. Ever."

"You're not the only one," Bart said, and we all voiced our agreement.

But the show wasn't over.

As Coach turned to the bench, he spotted a young man and his parents standing at the door to the dressing room—Lloyd and Mr. and Mrs. Blanton. Lloyd's dad had his arm wrapped around his son's waist, helping him walk to the bench. Mrs. Blanton walked beside her son and spoke quietly to him.

Coach clapped his hands and pointed to the Blantons.

Once more the crowd responded. They slowly rose to their feet, but this time it was to cheer the return of their newest favorite son, Lloyd Blanton. He never missed a practice, never made an excuse, always striving for a starting role. Striving to please his dad.

And now he was a hero.

"Lloyd," Coach said, "welcome back. I've been saving a place for you. If you'll sit next to me I'd be honored."

"Come on, Coach," Lloyd said with a shy smile.

"Son, take him up on it," Mr. Blanton said. "We'll sit right behind you, one row up in the bleachers."

"Let's play ball!" shouted the lead referee. "Who's shooting the technical foul shots, Coach?"

Coach tapped Jimmy on the shoulder, and he hit both shots.

Eagles 13–Panthers 11.

Next, we lined up as Johnny stepped to the line for his two free throws. Eagles 13–Panthers 13. Tie game!

We got the ball at midcourt because of the technical foul. The ref blew his whistle, tossed Bart the ball, and with one minute and forty-five seconds remaining in the first quarter, play began again.

With tough-man Danny gone for good, the fight drained out of the Eagles. They were still taller than we were. Still highly skilled basketballers.

But fight is everything.

Good, clean fight.

Their coach did all he could to inspire his players, hollering orders and running from one end of the bench to the other.

"Block out! How can you get a rebound if you don't block out!"

We threw a full-court press at them, and they were not ready. Jimmy stole an inbounds pass for an easy lay-up. Then Johnny jumped in front of their post man, grabbed the pass, and hit me running down the sideline.

If there was any doubt about Johnny's health, it quickly vanished. He outran all nine players, Eagles and Panthers both, and caught my lob pass for a dunk shot.

By halftime we were up by eight.

Panthers 35–Eagles 27.

As we trotted to the dressing room, I ran beside Jimmy. He was, after all, our senior leader. I wanted to show him some respect. "Pretty cool, huh?" I said.

"More than cool. Unbelievable. But we do have one big problem," he said, in a serious tone of voice.

"Yeah, we've got to keep the pressure on," I said. "Game's not over yet."

"That's not what I'm talking about."

"What, Jimmy?"

"After we kick hiney big time in the second half, there's no way we can have a team-only party after the game. Our parents are gonna have to join us. They'll follow us wherever we go. Get ready for some sentimental mom and dad hugs."

"Yeah, I guess you're right," I said laughing. "I never thought about that."

We were ready for Coach's talk. "I'm prouder of every one of you than you will ever know," he began. "You did not respond to their taunts, their dirty play. You played hard, clean basketball.

"And you are showing your maturity. Bart," he said, turning to the shyest senior on the team. "What have I not said?"

Bart stood up before he answered. "We can't be overconfident," he said, and his voice grew louder as he continued. "We won the first half, but the game is far from over. We have to hustle and fight and carry this win home!"

"Yeah!" we all shouted, as Bart looked at Coach for approval.

"I couldn't have said it better myself," Coach said.

We expected him to ask us to join hands before sending us back to the court. But this was a night of surprises, and one more awaited us.

"I have invited a guest to speak to you, so show him your respect," he said.

He opened the dressing room door and said, "The men are ready for you now."

Mr. Blanton stepped into the dressing room. The same Mr. Blanton who had threatened Coach with a chair and shattered his glass window.

CHAPTER 17

Standing at the Gates

He stood before us with a shy look on his face, one we'd never seen. He shook his head and glanced over at Coach.

"Oh, Coach," he said with a smile, "this is very strange. I feel a little like I'm standing at the Pearly Gates. But instead of Saint Peter deciding who gets to enter, I've got to convince a bunch of teenage boys that I'm worthy."

We all had to laugh at that one. Even Coach. Even Mr. Blanton.

"Give it a try," Coach Robison said.

"Alright," he began, turning back to us. "You are young men. Good young men. And I have always thought of myself as better than you. I was your boss. I didn't care a thing for how you felt or what you thought. I didn't give a damn.

"And as Lloyd grew up, I had to show him I was still the boss."

He paused and took a deep breath, looking again to Coach.

Coach nodded and gestured for him to continue.

"I woke up last Saturday morning in jail. And for the first time I looked at myself as others were seeing me. So I came here for two reasons. First, I want you to forgive me and give me another chance to be a part of my son's senior year.

"And second, I want you to win this game for your coach. He has opened my eyes that I might see. And boys," he added, "know that your mother and your father both love you, whether you win or lose. And what you do on the court does not—in spite of what everyone says—stay on the court. It carries over into the court of life, the real court.

"And never forget, the court of life begins the day you are born and continues till the day you die. You are given a name at birth. But you are also given a name that will stay with you, sometimes for many years after you have fought and struggled to leave it behind. They might call you hardworking. They might call you tough as nails. They might call you deaf, dumb, and blind. They might call you a fighter."

He paused and looked at Coach, took a deep breath, then continued. "They might call you a drunk. But never forget. You earned your name. They didn't make it up. You earned it. And all I am asking you to do tonight is *earn your name*. A name earned will never be forgotten."

Mr. Blanton closed his eyes and waved his hands in front of his face, unable to continue. We sat before him, as his whole life flooded the room.

Coach Robison gripped his shoulder and shook his hand.

"Never forget the words of this good man," he said. "Your life is carved by the choices you make. You earn your name by your actions."

"Thank you, Coach," he said, eyes closed and head bowed.

"I think you have earned a name, Mr. Blanton. The Choctaw word for tree is *iti,* and *chukma* means 'good.' And you, Mr. Blanton, are the strongest, stoutest tree we know. *Iti Chukma*, a good, strong tree."

He turned to us. "Say it with me, boys. Say it to Mr. Blanton. He has earned his name."

"Iti Chukma," we all said, nodding with respect at Lloyd's dad.

"I will try with all my strength to be worthy of this name," said Mr. Blanton.

"Now," Coach Robison said, "let's join hands and win this game. Mr. Blanton, please join us."

"Yeah!" we shouted, and on our way to the door, every Panther patted Lloyd's dad on the back and said good things to him.

"Nice going, Mr. Blanton."

"Glad you're with us."

"Lloyd has a good dad."

"You don't need our forgiveness, but you got it."

"Get Lloyd well. We need him back."

"Stay cool."

"Lloyd," Coach shouted, "lead us to the court. You and your family!"

Lloyd was now walking, or limping at least. As the crowd cheered to welcome him, his parents took their place in the bleachers above us. Soon the refs blew their whistles and the second half began.

"Keep up the pressure," Coach urged as we took the court.

We circled at midcourt for the tip, and my defender cross-stepped in front of me and shoved me aside.

"So we're gonna play that way," I said.

Johnny gave me a *what are you doing?* look.

Maybe I did step over the line, I thought. *Stay cool.* But I also knew that if that same "Eagles attitude" continued into the second half, we could beat these guys. They could push and shove, mouth off and hack, but take away their star player—they couldn't back it up.

Johnny lost the tip, and Jimmy's man grabbed the ball. He tossed the ball to their playmaker, who dribbled slowly across court.

"Play tight," Coach Robison shouted. We heard his real message.

They might try to slow the game down, but don't get lulled to sleep. We hustle on D and run when we have the ball.

Again they lobbed the ball to the post, ten feet from the bucket on the right baseline. Out of habit he turned, looking for Danny cutting under the hoop. But Danny was sitting on the team bus, listening to the game on the radio.

Their second-team post man tried to cut to the ball, but Jimmy intercepted and we dashed to our goal.

Panthers, Panthers! Go! Go! Go!

Our crowd was already into it, stomping and cheering. Jimmy hit me at midcourt, and I threw it to Johnny speeding in from the baseline. He caught the ball with one hand and fired it to Bart at the free-throw line. Bart missed, but Johnny got the tip-in.

I know we are fast, but when the game began, we were no match for the Eagles.

Where were they during our fast break?

Two Eagles were jogging downcourt, still arguing over whose fault it was, our intercepting the pass.

"Nice going, men!" Coach shouted. "Don't let up!"

By the end of the third quarter, we had extended the lead to twelve. Panthers 54–Eagles 42.

Then exhaustion set in. I found myself looking to the bench. My chest burned and I was puffing hard.

"Keep pushing!" Coach shouted, every time we touched the ball. Lloyd, Bart, and I could play either point or shooting guard, so we had time to catch our breath during every game. But we had no Lloyd.

This will take some getting used to, I thought. *Not good.*

"You gonna be hoke?" Coach asked as I ran by the bench.

"I'm fine," I lied.

Coach called a quick time-out.

"Men, we've got a nice lead. I'd love to tell you to keep running. That's how we built the lead. Let's drop back on the press. Pick 'em up at midcourt. Play tough, tight defense. Make them work for every shot. And when we get the ball, take some time off the clock. Walk the ball up court. That doesn't mean don't hustle. We clear on that?"

"Yes, sir!" we shouted.

What happened next came as no surprise.

Everybody in the gym could see we were exhausted. And we were a six-man team. Our bench players worked hard. But shooting the ball, dribbling the ball—hey, you can't have everything!

And how do you turn up the fire on a team with no bench?

Full-court press.

Yikes! Our ball under the Eagles basket. Bart, our shortest player, took the ball out of bounds. The long-armed Eagle post man waved his hands back and forth in Bart's face. I stepped out of bounds and called for the ball.

"Throw it to me!"

Bart flipped the ball to me, and I threw a long pass to Jimmy. He leapt high for the ball at midcourt and took one hard dribble, moving quick to the basket.

Cherokee Johnny suddenly appeared, to the joy of Coach.

"Yo, Jimmy!" he called out, lifting his arms to the ceiling. Jimmy got the message. He dribbled a slow step back and waited for me to cross half-court.

Slow it down. Run some clock. Protect our lead.

My man went for the steal, diving for the ball and hacking me on the wrist. He slapped hard, and my hand stung.

I'll feel that in the morning, I thought. Two free throws and nothing but net lessened the pain.

Standing at the Gates

The final quarter was the longest eight minutes of basketball I've ever played in my life. I had to remind myself that basketball is fun! Then my legs and back and lungs would scream, "Basketball is work!"

We finally pulled it out.

Panthers 68–Eagles 60.

"No partying tonight, men," Coach Robison announced after the game. "Let's take the weekend off, and I'll see you Monday. A great win tonight."

When he left the dressing room, I knew he was going to check on Lloyd and his dad. It was different celebrating a victory without Coach. Soon it became more than different. The assistant principal, Mr. Walters, entered through the coaches' office.

"Listen up!" he shouted. He didn't have to say it twice. "Coach Robison asked me to tell you that he won't be back this evening, so I'll stay and lock up."

We knew this meant hurry up, so we did. We got dressed and were soon saying our goodbyes in the parking lot.

"Hop in. Let's go," Johnny said, pulling his car to the curb.

"Not yet, Johnny. Go on if you want to. I'm not leaving yet."

"What's going on?" Johnny asked. He parked and joined me on the sidewalk.

"I've got a funny feeling," I said. "Something is just not right. Coach Robison's car is still here, but he's not. He was checking on Lloyd. I'm afraid something happened."

Less than five minutes later, a cab pulled to the curb and Coach Robison jumped out.

"I'm glad you boys are still here," he said. "Come get in my car. I'll call your parents. We're going to the hospital."

"Is Lloyd hurt bad?" I asked.

"Much worse," Coach said. "It's his dad."

CHAPTER 18

Candle in the Dark

We climbed in his car, buckled our seat belts, and waited. For way too long we waited. Coach sped through every yellow light and paid no attention to speed limit signs. This was not the Coach we knew.

He finally told us why.

"I walked with Lloyd and his parents to their car after the game. After he helped Lloyd into the back seat, his dad fell against the car. 'I'm hurting,' he said. Then he passed out, and I called 911."

Coach turned on his blinker and took a left onto the highway.

"I rode with him, Lloyd, and Mrs. Blanton in the ambulance to the hospital."

"Is he gonna be hoke?" Johnny asked.

Coach Robison took a deep breath and gripped the steering wheel with both hands. He shook his head back and forth, not wanting to hear his own words.

"He had a heart attack. He's in the emergency room now."

"How is Lloyd?" I asked.

"He is pacing up and down the waiting room, doing his best to hold it together. When he started sobbing, I grabbed him and buried his head in my chest. So they wouldn't ask him to leave."

"Is Mr. Blanton going to make it?" I asked.

More waiting.

Johnny reached over from the back seat and patted my shoulder. He was as scared as I was. For Lloyd.

"They were considering open-heart surgery when I left," Coach said. "I had to see if any of you boys had heard anything. I'm so glad you two waited. Lloyd needs you now more than ever."

"We are there for him, Coach," Johnny said.

I hesitated asking, but I had to know.

"And Heather?"

Coach laughed out loud and slapped the steering wheel. "Now that's a good question," he said, puffing his cheeks, blowing air, and leaning back, still laughing.

"Did I say something wrong, Coach?"

Coach glanced at me with a smile. "No, Bobby. You're just walking the Choctaw road. A little humor lightens the tragedy, achukma."

"Mind telling a less-informed Cherokee what you two are talking about?" Johnny asked.

"Heather, Lloyd's girlfriend. Yes. She was close by when Lloyd's dad fell. And so was Miss Popcorn."

"You mean Faye?"

"Oh, is that what you call her?" Coach asked. "I thought her Choctaw name was Miss Popcorn."

How can this be happening?

We all had to laugh at that one.

"Yes," Coach continued, and his voice took on a serious tone. "Heather was there. She waited till the ambulance arrived and ran for her car, to follow us to the hospital. Faye was still standing on the sidewalk, looking back and forth at the action all around her. She didn't know what to do.

"Heather pulled up to the curb and grabbed her arm. 'You're coming with me!' she shouted. So we all drove away together."

"And now?"

"Heather and Faye are sitting together in the waiting room."

"That reminds me of something Dad used to say," I said.

"I know," Coach said. "I heard him say it a hundred times at the bar. Usually after a kickoff return or an interception runback for a touchdown. He'd take a swig of beer and say, 'The good Lord takes a strange path, His miracles to perform.' Is that it, Bobby?"

"That's close," I said.

We soon arrived at the hospital. Coach parked in the "Emergency Room Only" parking lot and hurried us inside. There was a crowd in the waiting room, friends and family of the Blantons. They were well known and well liked.

Lloyd was lingering in the hallway by himself.

"Say hello to your friends, Lloyd," Coach said, then stepped into the waiting room to leave us alone.

"How's it going, Lloyd?" I asked.

"Open-heart surgery," he said. "They've already wheeled him away."

Nothing to say.

Nothing would make this right.

So we did something teenage boys never do. Never.

We huddled together in a warm, arm-wrapping hug.

Till we couldn't breathe.

"Can I call Jimmy and Darrell? And Bart too?" I asked. "We need our starting six—here and together."

Johnny made the call.

"Are they on their way?" I asked.

"Yes. Jimmy agreed to pick the others up. They should be here soon."

"Had they heard anything?" Lloyd asked.

"No. They were as shocked as we were. But they're coming."

Coach stepped from the waiting room and motioned to Lloyd. "The head surgeon wants to meet with the family," he said. "They're waiting for you."

We followed him to the waiting room and watched as he stepped through the doors labeled "Medical Personnel Only."

Twenty or more people crowded into the tiny space. No one said a word. I lowered my head and let my eyes gaze around the room. A married couple squeezed each other's hands and stared straight ahead. An elderly lady buried her face in a handkerchief, sobbing quietly.

When Lloyd shouted, everyone jerked and looked back and forth, looking for answers.

"Noooo! You can't give up. He is my father. He is not dead!"

Coach stood and approached the door, but he never entered. Lloyd flung the doors open and half ran through the waiting room, banging his fist against the door as he dashed to the hallway.

We followed Coach to the hall, then paused.

Jimmy, Bart, and Darrell held Lloyd. "The doctor said there is very little chance that Dad will live. He has blockage in every artery going to his heart," Lloyd said. No crying. His face sported a determined look.

I glanced at Coach and saw the pride in his face as he bowed his head and closed his eyes. Heather soon joined us, followed by Faye.

"Please," said Coach. "Everyone wait here. I will be back in a moment." He approached the nurses' station. After a brief conversation, he was motioned down the hall.

Ten minutes later he returned.

"They are continuing treatment to flush out the arteries," he said. "We may know soon, I was told. But it could take hours."

"Coach," Lloyd said. "The surgeon who spoke to us seemed to have no hope. And I know I should never holler in a hospital. That's the kind of thing my dad would do. But something changed when I did. The doctor got that same look that you have, when it looks like we don't have a chance."

"There is always a chance," Coach said.

"Yes. And Dad deserves another one."

"Johnny," Coach said, "can you take the first watch?"

"Sure, Coach. What do you want me to do?"

"Go back to the waiting room. Stay close to the door to surgery. If the doctor calls for the family, call Lloyd immediately."

"Yes, sir."

After the longest hour of Lloyd's life, his phone finally rang. It was Johnny.

"Will you say that again?" Lloyd asked. "I want to put you on speaker phone."

"Be glad to," Johnny said. "Lloyd, the surgeon says your dad would like to speak to you."

"I'm on my way," Lloyd said, leaving us behind in his full-speed sprint to the basket.

"Looks like his ankle has healed," Jimmy said.

We hurried down the hall, only to be met by another miracle.

My dad stood holding the door open for us.

"The Lord works in mysterious ways, His wonders to perform," Dad said.

CHAPTER 19

First Time for Everything

Lloyd's dad proved to be as strong as a tree—*Iti Chukma*, a good tree. Soon after Lloyd hurried through the doors for a few words with his dad, the surgeon appeared. He removed his gloves and handed them to an aide. When he turned to us he took a deep breath and shook his head back and forth, an adult way of saying, "I'm not believing this."

We waited.

"Mr. Blanton has severe blockage in the left descending artery," he said, "and he's very fortunate. We have inserted a stent to restore blood flow, and he should be fine. We'll keep a close watch on him, monitor his heart rate, and check vital signs. All things going well, he'll be discharged and soon begin cardiac rehab."

"How long will he remain in the hospital?" Coach asked.

"He should stay in intensive care for several more days. And I might add, I am giving you this medical information because Mrs. Blanton asked me to. Otherwise, it would be for family only."

"We appreciate it, Doctor," Coach said, shaking his hand for all of us. "We feel like family."

Lloyd soon stepped through the doors, with his arms wrapped around himself and his head down. "He's gonna make it," he said, without looking up. "My dad will live to see me play another game."

We encircled him, as if the game were tonight, as if we were about to dash to the court for the opening tip-off.

"Next game," Lloyd said, "let's win one for my dad, Iti Chukma. He has earned his name, and he just did something I'll never forget. He told me he loved me."

Lloyd looked up at us with watery eyes.

"He never did that before."

About the Author

Tim Tingle is an Oklahoma Choctaw and an award-winning author and storyteller. Every Labor Day, Tingle performs a Choctaw story before the Chief's State of the Nation Address, a gathering that attracts over ninety thousand tribal members and friends.

In June 2011, Tingle spoke at the Library of Congress and presented his first performance at the Kennedy Center in Washington, DC. From 2011 to 2016, he was a featured author and storyteller at Choctaw Days, a celebration at the Smithsonian's National Museum of the American Indian honoring the Oklahoma Choctaws.

Tingle's great-great-grandfather, John Carnes, walked the Trail of Tears in 1835. In 1992, Tim retraced the Trail to Choctaw homelands in Mississippi and began recording stories of tribal elders. His first book, *Walking the Choctaw Road*, was the outcome. His first children's book, *Crossing Bok Chitto*, garnered over twenty state and national awards and was an Editor's Choice in the *New York Times* Book Review. *Danny Blackgoat: Navajo Prisoner*, Tim's first PathFinders novel, was an American Indian Youth Literature Awards Honor Book in 2014.

PathFinders novels offer exciting contemporary and historical stories featuring Native teens and written by Native authors. For more information, visit: NativeVoicesBooks.com

Tim Tingle's *No Name* series is the story of Bobby Byington, a Choctaw teen who is proud to be a starter on his high school basketball team but whose personal life is filled with turmoil. Basketball and friendship are driving forces, as Bobby and his friends deal with parental alcoholism, school bullies, and prejudice.

No Name
978-1-93905-306-0 • $9.95

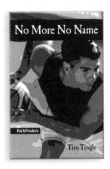

No More No Name
978-1-93905-317-6 • $9.95

A Name Earned
978-1-939053-18-3 • $9.95

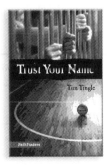

Trust Your Name
978-1-939053-19-0 • $9.95
Available July 2018